CHRISTMAS DREAMS

Mistletoe Meadows
Book 4

JESSIE GUSSMAN

Contents

Acknowledgments

Cover art by Covers and Cupcakes
Editing by Heather Hayden
Narration by Jay Dyess
Author Services by CE Author Assistant

Listen to the unabridged audio for FREE performed by Jay Dyess on the Say with Jay channel on YouTube. Get early access to all of Jay's recordings and listen to Jessie's books before they're available to the general public, plus get daily Bible readings by Jay and bonus scenes by becoming a Say with Jay channel member.

Chapter One

Gilbert McBride pushed away from his desk and leaned back in his chair, putting his hands behind his head and looking up at the ceiling.

He'd done it. Finally. After more than a year of relentless work and effort, blood, sweat, and tears, he had brought his equipment rental business back from the brink of bankruptcy and turned it into a profitable business machine once more.

His wife's cancer and subsequent death had almost ruined it. Not just because all of Gilbert's energy was fixated on being with his wife and children during that difficult time, but because his office manager had been embezzling money. She offered discounts to people who paid in cash, then pocketed the cash, not mentioning it in the books, of course, and hadn't paid any of the monthly bills.

By the time his lifelong friend had been propositioned by her, the company was on the verge of going belly up. That was just about the time that Gilbert's wife had died.

That was Christmas, one year ago.

In the last year, he worked relentlessly, building things up again, because he felt he owed it to his three children to provide as stable of a home as he could. Granted, in the last year, he hadn't been around much, but they had been well taken care of by his mother, who had raised six children of her own and could certainly handle three more.

It was true he felt guilty, but he also felt like he had no choice. If he was going to be a good father and provide for them, he had to do something to save his business, and it was going to have to be radical, and he was going to have to be all in.

But he knew if he put a whole lot of effort into it and gave himself a year, he could get the ship righted, and then once that happened, he would have time to spend with his children again.

The profit from last month would enable him to have a sizable down payment to put on a house, they could move out of his mother's place, and he and his children would become a family again.

He hadn't wanted to do it that way, but he hadn't seen any other way to save the business and his family. Losing the business would have meant being in debt for the rest of his children's childhoods, and he hadn't wanted that stress on his family. Losing their wife and mother had been enough.

He knew that there were people who criticized him for not being there for his children after their mother's death. He had taken two full weeks to spend entirely with them before he plunged himself into the business, but...he couldn't do both. And while his children were more important than any business, he also was commanded to be the provider for his family. He couldn't just let that go, as much as he might have wanted to hold each one of his children close for as long as he could.

His phone buzzed and he sat up, grabbing it from off the desk where he'd set it, and saw that it was his realtor calling. He'd put in a request last week for a farm, preferably one that could raise horses, since the therapy riding that they'd done seemed to make his children happy, and he wanted it in the general area where his mother and siblings lived in Mistletoe Meadows. Ideally, he had told his realtor, he wanted to be moved in by Christmas. Considering that it was currently October, he thought he might have been a little bit demanding, but in his experience, it was best to say what he actually wanted, rather than settling. Who knew, maybe the Lord would open the door and see fit to bless him and his children with the perfect location.

"Hello?" he said, standing up out of his chair and walking around until he stood in front of the window, looking out on the buildings of Harrisonburg, Virginia. It was a nice town but bigger than what he was used to, and there was no need for him to stay, now that the business was in hand.

He could go back to Mistletoe Meadows where he really wanted to be.

"Gilbert. I'm so glad I caught you. You know what a tight market we're in right now, and I told you when you gave me your dream list that more than likely we'd not be able to find anything, but...I am very pleased to inform you that I have advance knowledge of a farm, just like you asked for, coming onto the market. It should be listed later today or tomorrow at the latest. And it's currently being used as a horse therapy facility, so horses are definitely a centerpiece."

"Just like I requested," he said, feeling very satisfied. He put a hand on the wall and leaned against it, looking off at the brilliant blue October sky. "You can send me the information, but I trust that you found what I wanted. I'll go see the property as soon as you can arrange it, and I'll come prepared to make an offer on the spot."

He had everything lined up and did not intend to dillydally around. He wanted to get his family back together. He didn't want to bring his children back to Harrisonburg, putting them back in school there, when he knew he was going to be moving them and wouldn't have time to be mom and dad while he rescued his business, so they had spent a lot of time at his mother's house. It was also good for the kids to be out in the country where they could run around versus the town home that his late wife had preferred.

That had already sold, which is what had given him the money to help bring his business back in the black and eventually what had enabled him to get the down payment for the farm he intended to purchase.

Still, the downside had been that he hadn't been able to have his children with him since he'd been sleeping in the apartment above the shop, except on weekends and occasionally during the week when he was able to make the drive to Mistletoe Meadows.

"I've already done it. I have us scheduled for a showing tomorrow morning at nine AM. If that doesn't suit, I can reschedule. Just let me know."

"That's perfect."

He made a mental note to talk to his new office manager. The man had come highly recommended, and Gilbert intended to oversee everything. He had no wife to get cancer or, before that, to cheat on him.

His lips pressed together. No one knew about that. He hadn't told a soul about the letter that he found that had changed everything between his wife and him.

"All right. I'll see you bright and early tomorrow morning," she said before they said goodbye and hung up.

He texted his office manager immediately, letting him know that he would be in late in the morning if at all.

Sending the text off, he leaned against the wall and contemplated all the things that he needed to do. He felt like the business was a priority, but now that it was taken care of, his children were going to take center stage. Lucas was almost thirteen, which was a delicate age, and he needed his father.

Gilbert had spent as much time with him as he could over the summer, but he appreciated his brother-in-law helping out as well. Especially when he couldn't be there.

Then there was Larissa, who followed her grandmother around everywhere and thought the woman walked on water. Gilbert wasn't entirely sure that his mother didn't walk on water. She seemed to be almost perfect. Young for her age, and resourceful, although she was definitely moving slower and getting older. He didn't like to think about it, because his mother had been the one constant in his life. The person he could always depend on to do right and to be there for him. When his wife was in the hospital, his mother dropped everything to do whatever he needed her to—watch the kids, make food, give him a ride if he needed it, whatever it was, whatever he asked, she never said no. He owed her so much more than he could ever repay.

And then there was Robert, who was ten and somewhat quiet. Gilbert didn't know him as well, but he had every intention of changing that, and soon.

Chapter Two

"Just sign right here, ma'am, and I'll take care of everything else."

Summer Lubbock picked up the pen and held her breath. She sat in the real estate office with her agent, Frederick, sitting across from her. He had drawn up the contract that laid out their fees and stipulations that she had to sign in order for them to list and sell her property.

The farm had been in her family for generations, and she hated that she was losing it, but she didn't have much choice. Her parents had mortgaged it, and then when real estate prices went down, they were underwater. She had done everything she could to try to earn money to continue to pay the mortgage, but she'd slowly and surely gotten more and more behind.

Then, when her prized Paso Fino horse had developed colic, and she'd sent her to Virginia Tech to have surgery, she'd been slapped with a $35,000 bill.

There was no way she could pay it and keep current on the mortgage. She was doing her best to chip away at both, but at this point, she knew it was time. She should have just put the horse down, but she had hoped that she would be able to save her, not just since she was pregnant and the foal would have been worth almost as much as the surgery cost, but because she loved her.

But she'd lost the mare, the foal, and now the farm.

She wasn't very good at placing bets.

Definitely she should stay well away from Las Vegas.

She rolled her eyes, exhaled, and scribbled her name on the line.

"Excellent. I'll get your farm listed. I'll get all the information typed in, and the listing should be up online today or at the very latest tomorrow. I'll send a memo around in-house to let all of our current agents know, so they can alert any potential buyers that they have waiting in the wings looking for property just like yours. It is a beautiful place."

Summer nodded. She knew he was right. Her mother had mortgaged the place so she could remodel, and she had done a beautiful job. The house looked like a showpiece, with huge windows, skylights everywhere, and all brand-new and modern designs. The kitchen was her favorite. It was huge, with a big island and plenty of natural light. Summer had plants and candles sitting around, and the place always brought her comfort and peace and joy.

But no matter how much comfort and peace and joy it gave her, those things didn't pay the bills. She could cook, but she wasn't a great at it, and as the farm sank further and further into debt, she spent less and less time in the kitchen and more and more time trying to take care of her current clients and to get more. But no matter how hard she worked, it wasn't enough.

"All right, there's probably going to be a good bit of activity here at the beginning when the listing first goes up as buyers in that price range book showings. I would go home and make sure everything's in tip-top shape, because I wouldn't be surprised if you have several shows this week."

"All right, thanks. You're sure it'll be okay if I continue to work outside while people are viewing the property?"

"It's always best if the owner is completely off the property while it's being shown, but if you're working, and you can't stop, there's not a whole lot we can do. However, my highest recommendation is that you vacate the premises if at all possible."

"All right." He had already said that, but she had explained to him that she worked on the property and couldn't just cancel her clients because someone wanted to come see it. That was how she made her money, and until the farm sold, she needed to continue making an income.

After the farm sold... Then she had to sell her horses, which made her heart clench and she couldn't spend more than a couple of seconds thinking about it. And then... She supposed she'd have to see how much money she had left after paying the mortgage off, whether it would be enough for a down payment on a smaller facility, or whether she would have to sell all of the horses and move somewhere to a smaller place with no barn or acreage.

Her degree in counseling gave her a little bit of a cushion. She could open her own practice, although from experience, she knew that starting her own business took a lot of time, money, and effort, and patience as she waited for word of mouth to get out, since that was the best advertisement—satisfied patients.

Regardless, she didn't think she was going to starve to death, and she would just do the best she could.

Walking out of the real estate office, she blinked in the bright sunlight. The street seemed busier than usual, and she remembered that Mistletoe Meadows was having their a Christmas festival tomorrow. Because of their Christmas-like name, they had Christmas festivals year-round.

She had signed up to have two horses in the parade.

Back when she had originally signed up, she had hoped that one of the horses would have been Princess Sugarcube, who had just passed away.

She blew out a breath and turned left toward her car, thinking that perhaps she would stop in at Sunny's bakeshop and grab a muffin since she wasn't going to have time to do breakfast before her first client.

She didn't typically have a whole lot of clients during the day, since most of her clients were children, and she saw them after school.

She smiled, thinking of her favorite clients, the McBride children, with whom she had been working for free for the last year. Their mother had died of cancer, and their father had neglected the business during her illness to the point where he almost lost it. From what she understood, he had spent a lot of time the last year trying to get solvent again.

She hoped he was able to, since, although she didn't know Mr. McBride very well, his children were the sweetest and she wanted the best for them.

Especially Larissa, who wanted to be a horsewoman when she grew up, although she didn't really know exactly in what way. She just wanted to work with horses. But she was only ten, and it didn't matter. She just knew that she loved horses and wanted to spend every waking second she could with them.

Summer had spent a lot of time above and beyond the therapy time, showing Larissa everything she wanted to know and allowing her to follow Summer around as she cleaned the stables, took care of the horses, and occasionally exercised them. She was even there when the farrier and vet came to work on the animals. Larissa had been an angel, and Summer hated to see her time with her come to an end, but it almost certainly would. The odds of her being able to sell the farm and buy another place anywhere close to Mistletoe Meadows were very slim.

"Hey, Summer," Sunny greeted her as she walked into the bakeshop, which was on the downside of the busy time of morning.

"Good morning," Summer said, grinning at her friend.

"What brings you to town today? Feed run?" Sunny said with her normal smile. In addition to the bakeshop, she also played violin in a trio that often performed in the area. Summer wasn't sure whether the cello or baking was her true passion, since she seemed to be equally passionate about both.

"No. I signed the papers at the real estate office to put the farm up for sale. It should be hitting the MLS later today or tomorrow, Frederick said."

"You're selling the farm?" Sunny stopped bustling around behind the counter and focused on Summer. "Really?"

"Yeah," Summer said, hating the ache that seemed to reverberate through her chest.

"But it's been in your family for generations."

"I know."

"Is it because of your mom and her renovations?"

"Mostly. I've been chipping away at the mortgage, but when Princess had her surgery this summer, I just...couldn't do it all. And I probably should have let the surgery go unpaid, but that was going to get turned into a bill collector too. I just...can't do it." She lifted her shoulder. She didn't want to go into all the details, all of the bills that her parents had left. It wasn't just the mortgage, and it was far more than one person could afford to pay. She wasn't even sure when she sold the farm whether she would be out from underneath everything.

She hoped so; with the amount that they were asking, she'd be free and clean with a little something left. Probably not enough to buy another farm, but enough to live somewhere.

But if the buyer tried to get her to come down on her price, she could be left with nothing.

"Here, have a blueberry muffin." Sunny grabbed the muffin and a napkin and set them on top of the display case. "I'm not selling these today, since I just tried a new recipe. I was trying to get a little crumbly crunch on top. You can let me know if I did okay. I want the inside to be nice and moist."

"Are you sure?" Summer asked with her brows raised. She didn't come into her friend's shop to get handouts. And she hadn't told her tale of woe because she was hoping to get something out of it. Sunny had asked.

"Yes. I'm positive. All the payment I require is your opinion on how they taste and what the texture is like."

"All right." She took the blueberry muffin and took a bite out of the top, chewing and swallowing before she spoke. "That's perfect. That's a great, almost crunchy top, but it's very moist and chewy in the middle. I say it's a keeper."

"All right. Three votes yes, one vote no so far today."

"Oh my goodness, who voted no?"

"Mrs. Tucker. She said they were too...sinful, I think that was her word."

"Oh. Well, I think maybe you could throw her vote out," Summer said before taking another bite. They were so good.

Summer didn't have any beef with Mrs. Tucker, although she was known as the town busybody. Summer figured that she just tried to keep things going in the town, and every small town needed a few people like that, people who pushed others to help out, to keep all the things that made a small town fantastic going.

That was Mrs. Tucker's position, for sure, and there were various people who ran when they saw her coming, but Summer had never crossed her.

"I've been thinking about it. It does seem for now that she is the only dissenting vote, and it wasn't because it didn't meet my standards. It was because it didn't meet hers."

They laughed a little together before Summer thanked her and left, walking to her truck and getting in. She shoved the rest of the muffin into her mouth and figured that would tide her over until she had a break around two or so that afternoon and could grab a bite to eat in the kitchen.

On the way home, she thought about all the time she'd spent on the farm. Growing up, the family get-togethers they used to have there, until the family went all of their different directions after her parents died, and the good memories that were still associated with it. She'd never lived anywhere else and really didn't want to.

Although, the house was big, far bigger than what a single woman needed. With six bedrooms, each of them completely redone and beautifully appointed. Her mom had even taken the seventh bedroom and turned it into two bathrooms so that there were three master bedrooms and three bedrooms that shared a bath.

The downstairs was just as nice, and her mother had entertained there for a while before she died. Her father passed away in a freak accident while riding a horse on the farm, and her mother passed away not long after. Some people said it was because of a broken heart, but Summer figured it was probably because of the financial stress.

She doubted her mother knew exactly what kind of financial issues they were having until after her husband passed away and it was her job to take care of it.

It certainly had been a big blow to Summer, but she'd shouldered it and had been carrying it for the last five years. But it was just more than she could do.

Regardless, she would need to start thinking about telling her clients, although who knew when the house would sell. Fredrick had indicated he thought it would go pretty quickly, but that was probably the job of a real estate agent, to be the cheerleader and the optimistic one. Summer knew some houses had sat on the market for years without selling, until someone had purchased them. So she wasn't holding her breath. Although, maybe it would be best to just have it happen fast.

Lord, help me to be okay with Your timing. Fast or slow. I could go either way. And You know what's best.

She had been raised to be a worker, someone who put their heart into everything they did. Sometimes it was hard to leave things in the Lord's hands, although when there was nothing left to do, she didn't have much choice. That was the point she was at.

She came up on the farm, seeing the For Sale sign, unfamiliar and out of place, sitting at the end of the drive.

She tried to fight back the sting of tears that threatened and swallowed hard. This was for the best. Sometimes it seemed like when things had gone as badly as they could, that's when everything broke loose and the good stuff started to happen.

She just had to let the farm go in order for God to open up His windows of blessing on her.

If only it was that easy.

But she also knew God didn't want her to be attached to earthly things. He wanted her to have her sights set on heaven. Her earthly home shouldn't mean as much to her as her heavenly home, and she shouldn't put as much store in it as she did in the treasure she stored in heaven.

Maybe that was the lesson the Lord wanted her to learn.

She just wished there was a less painful way to learn it.

Chapter Three

"I have an appointment tomorrow to go look at a farm. It's near here, and it just might be the one. The house is gorgeous, the grounds are perfect. There aren't too many acres, but we don't need a whole pile of ground, just enough to keep a couple of horses for the kids to ride. I'm not looking to grow crops or anything." Gilbert ran a hand through his hair, then put an elbow on the counter in front of him. He sat in his mother's kitchen, talking to her while she stood on the other side, baking a batch of cookies for the kids to eat when they got home from school that day.

"All right. But tomorrow is the festival. I know the kids would really like to go see the parade."

"I think we'll make it in time. The festival starts at eleven, and the parade is at one, right?"

"I think so. What time is your appointment to see the property?"

"It's nine. I don't think it'll take more than an hour, and honestly I'm going to get it, unless there's something majorly wrong with it. It's exactly what I want, and it's less than fifteen minutes from here."

"Wonder which property it is?" his mother mused.

"My agent said it just came on the market. In fact, it wasn't even listed as of yesterday, so you might not have heard about it."

"I can only think of a couple that could potentially be what you're talking about, although none of them have a really big house. How many bedrooms did you say?"

"I think there's six. Three with master bedrooms."

"Wow. And you said they're all in good shape?"

"Yeah. Apparently the woman who owned it, which is the mother of the current owner, from what I understand from my realtor, got the farm into debt redoing the house. She did a great job on the house, but the girl just can't keep up with the payments. That's the extra info that my realtor texted me last night. I'm not sure if that's general info that everyone knows."

"Goodness," his mom said, coming over to the counter and putting her hand on it. She didn't look happy, which Gilbert didn't really understand. He was coming home. He would get to spend time with his children. And he found the perfect property. Why could she be upset about that?

"That sounds like Summer Labach's place."

"Summer? Do I know her?"

"I think she was a good bit younger than you in school. It's the Labach farm. Where your kids go for horse therapy."

"Oh." Gilbert sat back, his feet hooked on the bottom rungs, his mind whirling.

There was no doubt in his mind that the horseback riding therapy had been beneficial for all three of his children. They all loved it and loved their instructor, although he wasn't sure if it was Summer or not. He never took them. Someone from his family always dropped them off and picked them up. He had been busy working in Harrisonburg.

"In fact, if I'm thinking about this right, I don't think she's charged us for the last year of therapy. Starting from before Desire passed, she had told me it was on the house. She and Larissa seemed to develop a bond, and she's been out there an awful lot. In fact, I think Larissa is riding in the parade tomorrow."

"Are you serious?" Now he felt bad. The woman had to sell her property because she couldn't afford to pay for it, and she hadn't even been charging him for the horseback riding therapy his kids had been taking. The thought that he hadn't been paying for it never even crossed his mind. He…just assumed everything was being taken care of, that it was automatically deducted from his checking account.

He sighed. "I guess that is sad."

"Yeah. It's been in her family for generations. I don't even know how long. But I know Summer is excellent with the children and very good at what she does. She's busy all summer long, and she's even run some camps. But from what I understand, she had a sick horse or something, and it put her back further than what she could catch up."

"Animals are expensive." He had wanted to get a dog for his kids. It wasn't the expense that kept him back, it was the fact that he hadn't had time. But when they moved out to the farm, that was something that he had wanted to get. He really wasn't into horses. Never had been, but he understood that some people were, and he also saw with his own eyes how much being around the horses had helped his children. He wasn't going to try to deny that.

The timer on the oven went off, and his mother went over, put an oven mitt on, and opened the door. The kitchen soon smelled absolutely delicious, and Gilbert's mouth started to water. He needed to get in better shape though, because while he put all of his effort into building his business, he neglected his health. And he'd definitely gained some weight. Of course, he figured moving to the farm would help with that as well.

"I think my kids are going to be spoiled. They're going to expect to walk into a kitchen that smells like baking cookies and have a warm tray of the same sitting on the counter waiting for them.

They're going to be disappointed when we move out and that doesn't happen anymore."

"Larissa is an excellent little baker. I think she might be excited to get her own kitchen. And I remember Mrs. Labach threw some wonderful parties. I was in the kitchen a couple of times, and it's gorgeous. Larissa will not be disappointed."

"Well, I can't thank you enough, because I know she didn't learn to bake from Desire."

He clamped his mouth closed over anything more. He always tried to say only the very best things about Desire. He didn't want to dishonor her memory in any way. He wanted his children's memories of her to be happy. After all, she was their mother, and they didn't need to know that she was a cheater. He had gotten over it himself. If she hadn't been diagnosed with cancer, it's possible that they would have gotten divorced, but in his eyes, God had saved his children from that, and now it was up to Gilbert to keep the secret.

"It's been a joy and a pleasure to have the children. Honestly, I'm a bit sad that you're going to take them. I mean, don't get me wrong, I'm thrilled that you're going to be home so much more and the children are going to see you. They need that so much. But... The house is going to seem so empty without them."

"You have Isadora."

"True."

Isadora and her three children were napping currently. Isadora had had her baby in March, and it had been a healthy baby girl. She had gotten her divorce finalized in June. Those had been hard months for her, and she still struggled now, in October.

"She's not doing so great," Gilbert said.

"People said the same thing about you last year this time. And pretty much all year. Not everyone understood why you had to spend so much time away from your children, and they talked."

"I figured they would. But I had to be able to support my family. It's my job to provide."

"I know, son." His mother put up her hand. "You don't need to talk to me about it. I supported you all the way. I did feel bad for your children, but you were in an impossible situation. With the embezzlement that had gone on, plus the neglect from you taking such great care of your wife… Something had to give. And I think you made the right choice, keeping the kids in the school system here and leaving them with me. I am not perfect, but I did the best I could, and I don't think anyone ever loves like a grandmother does."

"You could be right about that. Although, I love those kids pretty fiercely myself."

"I know you do. And now, it's your time. So, I'll be a little bit sad, but I know I'll see you guys again and plenty. And you know you're welcome here anytime."

"We'll have to establish a regular game night or something. That way, you can look forward to it, but it won't overwhelm you. You do deserve to have a little bit of a rest."

"If God wants me to rest, He can take me to heaven, and I'll rest there. But as long as I'm here on earth, God has work for me to do, and I'm going to do it with everything I have."

His mother put a cookie on a plate and set it in front of him without asking if he wanted one.

He couldn't resist a warm chocolate chip cookie, so he picked it up and started eating. But he was going to get back in shape, lose some weight, spend more time with his children, and…do all the things that he knew he should do but hadn't had time for the last year.

He did admire his mom. She lived what she believed better than anyone he knew. He hoped when his children got older, they could see the same thing about him.

Chapter Four

"Are you ready for the tour?" Jane asked as Gilbert got out of his car and met her at the front of the house.

"I've been looking forward to it," he said honestly. He hadn't said anything to his children the night before. He figured that if some of them were up this morning, he might invite them to go, but they were all sleeping in, so he let it go. He didn't want them to get their hopes up for nothing. After all, there might be something wrong with this property. He wasn't going to buy a property that needed a lot of attention.

Also, the words that his mother had said had spun around his head the night before. They loved Summer, their counselor, and he wasn't sure how they would feel about buying this property. Excited or aghast. Either way, he didn't want to deal with the reactions until it was a reality or at least until he was sure he was going to be putting an offer on it.

Of course, he told Jane to come prepared to write up an offer for him, because if he liked it, he was going to jump on it. In this market, properties didn't stay for sale long before they got snapped up. And he wasn't going to lollygag around.

"All right then, let's get started."

He glanced to the right, where, beyond the barn, a woman with a long blonde ponytail worked with a really pretty horse. Not that he knew anything about horses, he just knew this one was nice to look at. And she seemed to know what she was doing, as it trotted around in a circle with her holding some kind of rope.

She didn't look up at him, and he watched her for a couple of seconds without fear of being found out. It was like she was deliberately ignoring them.

"That's the owner, Summer Labach," Jane said in a whisper, as though the woman could hear her, despite the fact that there was probably one hundred yards between them. "The info on the property says that she will vacate the premises for showings if she can, but she makes her living from working on the farm. So she can't leave just any time. I believe she is a horseback riding therapist."

"Yeah. I didn't know if that was her or not. My kids have been in therapy here for more than a year, since before my wife died. Obviously I never brought them here."

"Oh, I'm so sorry. I didn't realize you'd lost your wife." Jane truly looked distressed, and he figured that she must have thought he was a divorced dad, since he showed up without a wife beside him.

He supposed that would have been the most logical assumption, but it wasn't true in his case.

If Desire had lived, it might have been. Although... He wouldn't have wanted to divorce her. When he said for better or for worse, he meant it. But she didn't forsake all others, apparently.

He shook himself and listened as Jane said, "The place is profitable, from what I understand. She just had so much back debt, and then she had one big vet bill this year that threw everything into chaos. It's sad, but that's the way life is."

"I heard it was in her family for a long time."

"It has been. They can trace it back to the late 1700s. Of course, it didn't look like it does today, and the original house is not still standing, but part of the house we're about to tour was built in the early 1800s, and everything else was added a little bit at a time, the way Southern homes often are. It's a hodgepodge of different architectural types and has a uniqueness all its own. Lots of character," Jane said, and he refrained from rolling his eyes. That sounded like something she would have to say. After all, she was trying to sell the place.

It was code for the place is a mess.

Although, when they walked into the foyer, Gilbert thought he might have to change that line of thought. It was wide open, bright, and airy. The floor was a light blue sandstone tile, and the stairs were a beautiful honey-colored hardwood. The banister looked like it was hand carved a hundred and fifty years ago when people still did that kind of thing, and the hall was wide and spacious.

"Obviously, a really big foyer," Jane said, deciding to go for understatement, apparently. "Over here is a formal living room, there is also a sitting room, an office, a den, a massive kitchen, and a laundry room as well as a full bath downstairs. Let's see if we can find them," she said, giggling a bit like she loved this kind of thing. Which would make sense, since she was a real estate agent and it was her job.

He walked into the formal living room which looked like it hadn't been used in months, if not years. The drapes were drawn, and while the windows looked big, there wasn't much light coming through. The chairs were formal and uncomfortable looking, there for show more than for comfort or for a sanctuary from the world.

It was a room he wouldn't use much if he bought the house, unless they completely redecorated it into...something that looked a little bit more livable.

The den looked cozy, although there wasn't much light, and there was a library of sorts, which Jane had failed to mention. It had shelves of books, which were full, along with a fireplace. He could see himself getting very comfortable in this room. While his job didn't demand much reading from him, he had always enjoyed a good thriller or adventure story.

He stepped into the kitchen, and he understood exactly what his mother had meant.

"Wow," he said, causing Jane to turn and smile at him.

"You can see why they were so far in debt they couldn't afford the payment on the farm. There was no expense spared in the remodeling of this area. Trust me, I've done a few remodeling projects, and those countertops are marble and the high-end kind. The cupboards are handcrafted, and I've heard that the pantry is the best pantry that Frederick, the listing agent, has ever seen."

She walked over to a small door and opened it.

Inside was a room almost as large as the kitchen, with shelves that reached from the ceiling to the floor. Most of them were empty, although he saw a package of paper plates, a crockpot, and several other large, bulky items that a person might need to use in the kitchen but would want to store somewhere else.

"My mom would love this," he murmured. She hadn't mentioned the pantry. Maybe she hadn't seen it.

The kitchen was airy and bright, and Summer had several plants growing. She must have a green thumb as well as being good with horses and children.

Poor kid, losing her home and everything she'd known. He felt a spark of pity for her, and it settled right beside the gratefulness that he felt for what she had done for his children. That, along with the knowledge that he had just found out the day before that she had not charged for her services for his children, made him feel a little guilty for walking around her house contemplating buying it out from underneath her.

But if he didn't, somebody else would.

But it didn't have to be him. It seemed like there were two factions inside his head that were warring against each other. One that thought that if he didn't buy the house, he was somehow doing Summer a favor. And the other trying to convince him that he might as well be the one to purchase it versus someone else.

"Let's go see what's upstairs. Shall we?" Jane tilted her head and waited for his assent.

The stairs were wide enough for both of them to easily walk side by side.

"They don't make staircases like this anymore."

"I can tell that the house was kind of cobbled together, but the way it was redesigned really makes it flow almost seamlessly." He wasn't quite sure how the designer was able to keep the idea that there were separate areas that flowed, but they did.

"I have to say, her designer was very talented. But since the woman spared no expense, I bet it was a big name from Richmond or even DC. I can only imagine it was the very, very best."

Gilbert nodded as he ascended the staircase.

The bedrooms were wide and well lit, with at least two windows in each. There was one that looked like it was being used, and he assumed it was Summer's bedroom. It wasn't the biggest room, and he guessed that it might have been the room that she'd had growing up, and maybe she had never moved into her parents' room once they had passed.

"Do you know what happened to her parents?" he asked, feeling a little bit bad for digging for information, but if it was common knowledge, she might as well tell him. All his mother knew was that they had died a while ago, and she thought the husband had died in a farming accident.

"The husband was thrown from a horse, hit his head on a rock, and broke his neck. He never regained consciousness." Jane looked down, as though sad to be relaying the sad news.

"And the wife?"

"She passed away not long after. Some say it was from a broken heart."

That was romantic. He could see his sisters saying that anyway.

"There's an attic, and you can go up if you'd like."

"I think I will, just to make sure the roof isn't leaking."

"It shouldn't be. It was replaced ten years ago. It's a metal roof and has a thirty-year lifespan."

"All right. I'll just check." It could have been leaking before they replaced it. He wasn't an expert, but he was going to do his due diligence to try to make sure that he didn't buy someone else's problems. It seemed obvious that the woman was selling because she had to. She needed the money, and couldn't afford the payments, and not because there was something wrong with the place, but he felt it would be wise to make sure.

It turned out that everything looked just fine up in the attic, although it was packed with things that looked like they'd been up there for years.

No doubt, Summer hadn't been up to go through things since her parents had died.

Someone was going to have a lot of junk to get rid of.

"There is also a basement, and then we can go outside and see the outbuildings," Jane said as they descended the stairs back down to the first floor. There was nothing interesting in the basement, other than a few jars of canned food and what looked like an area that someone had started to finish, possibly as a rec room, with a dry bar on one end, but had stopped mid project.

"It looks like this is what she was working on when her husband passed away," Jane said in passing.

Gilbert just nodded. He was wondering more and more about Summer. She obviously hadn't taken up the mantle of needing everything to look just right, and it seemed like maybe she had been focusing on trying to bring in enough money to pay for everything. At least that was the impression he was getting. It made him feel even worse for her. How hard it must be to struggle to keep a hold of your childhood home but be unable to.

Finally they were back out in the bright sunshine. A beautiful fall day that wasn't too warm. So nice after the hot, humid days of summer. The fresh, crisp air was a welcome change, along with the gentle breeze.

"There are only twenty acres with this, which makes it a little bit of a tough sell for anyone who is serious about horses. But for someone who just wants a few, it's the perfect amount of acreage."

"That's me," Gilbert said, just because Jane seemed to expect an answer, not because she didn't already know that.

They walked into the barn, and he noted that there were several animals in the stalls. Maybe filling up half of the ten available stalls.

Maybe he shouldn't have gone up to see the attic, because he hadn't made it halfway down the barn before Summer came in leading the horse she had been working with outside.

"Oh. I'm sorry. I didn't realize you hadn't made it out here."

"That's just fine, sweetie. You keep going about your business. Although... Gilbert, do you have anything to ask her?"

Chapter Five

*S*ummer almost walked back out the other side. She recognized Gilbert McBride, the father of her favorite therapy children. He'd lost his wife the previous Christmas, and she had felt so bad for him almost losing his business. She could totally relate to that since she was on the verge of losing her farm. That was one of the reasons she had not charged him for the therapy she had been giving his children for the last twelve months.

Talk about irony. She tried not to be bitter, but it just didn't seem fair that she had been working with his children, not charging him, while he had been building his business and had apparently been successful at it, since now he wanted to buy her farm, which she couldn't afford to keep.

No one could tell her that God didn't have a sense of humor.

"How many horses do you have?" he asked.

She blinked. She hadn't been expecting any prospective buyers to want to ask her anything. After all, that was why she hired a real estate agent, so they could sell the property. She'd answered all their questions, but...she supposed it made sense that he might have a few things he wanted to know. While she was answering, she wondered if he realized that he was talking to the person who gave his kids therapy. He'd never dropped them off or picked them up, and she doubted he recognized her. Although, his family might have told him that the farm was hers and her role in their lives. Did they tell him that she hadn't been charging him?

"I have five. I just lost one over the summer."

"And you give horseback riding therapy with those five horses?"

"I use three of them for my therapy. This one, and its buddy, are the ones I use for parades and for shows, and I hire them out at times as well." That was another angle where she was trying to make some money. That wasn't the only expense she had on the farm, putting the money into the horses. Of course, Princess had died and not only cost her all the money that she had put into her but left behind a huge vet bill as well.

It was over and done with, and not something she could fix, so there was no point in getting upset about it.

"My children take therapy from you."

"I know. I recognized you from seeing you last fall. I believe it was in town just before your wife passed away. I'm sorry." She'd seen him with his children at the grocery store. From what she understood, one of the rare times they'd been out together.

She did feel bad for him. From what she had heard, he had been completely devastated. At first, she had believed that other people had been bringing his children to therapy because he had been unable to function, but then word around town was that he had been rebuilding his business, which he almost lost because of neglect and embezzlement.

"You must have good eyes, if you remember me from that long ago."

"I do have a tendency to remember a face," she said. And a horse. She had that tendency too.

"Is there anything I should know about the place before I put an offer in?"

"I can't think of anything. Everything works just fine. I'm not selling because there is a huge list of repairs that need to be done. Of course, there are a few places in the fence that could be taken care of, but that's pretty much the way it always is. Animals scratch their necks or butts on it and bend it over and knock it down, and you're constantly repairing it unless you electrify it. Which I haven't done."

"I see. Everything's in pasture?"

He hadn't laughed at her statement about the animals with their necks and butts, and although she hadn't exactly meant it to be funny, because it was true, she said it with a smile. His face remained serious.

She kind of got the feeling that he might be a jerk. She wasn't sure what was giving her that vibe, but no doubt the guy did not seem to be overly friendly or nice, although he did keep asking her questions.

"Yes. I don't have any crops planted at all. Although I did get some hay off of ten acres twice this year. With only having five horses, they didn't eat all the grass. We had a good bit of rain this year. If it had been a dry year, I would have needed every bit of those twenty acres for them to eat, and then I would have bought hay this winter."

"So how many horses do you think this place could sustain comfortably?"

"In a wet year, it can easily handle the five horses that I have. In a dry year, you most likely couldn't have one, depending on how dry it was of course."

He nodded and then turned to his agent. "I think we can go." He looked back at Summer. "You'll be hearing from me. I love the place, and I'll be putting in an offer as soon as Jane can get it written up."

"All right. Sounds good," she said, feeling neither happiness nor animosity toward him. She didn't feel grateful either, although she supposed she probably should. His offer, if it was the full asking price, and it should be considering the place hadn't even been on the market for twenty-four hours, would enable her to be out of debt and no longer have the chains of debt wrapped around her.

She'd lived with it for so long she'd almost forgotten what it felt like to be free.

"Mr. McBride, you haven't seen the apartment that's above the stables. Would you like to look at that?" The real estate agent looked up from the papers she carried.

"Sure," he said, sounding surprised.

There wasn't much to see up there. Just two rooms, a kitchen and dining room and living room combo along with a bedroom, and a small bath with a standup shower. It had originally been built for a stable manager to stay, or if someone was on foal watch, they could hang out there too. The kitchen was tiny, although it did have a stove and a fridge, and the bathroom was serviceable, but it certainly was nothing compared to the house. She wouldn't rent it out to anyone. It just wasn't nice enough for someone to want to pay to stay there or to even turn it into a rental for a little bit of extra income. It would need to have some money poured into it first.

That was only her opinion though, and maybe she was wrong. She'd been wrong about a lot of things in her life, and that could be another one.

She glanced at her phone. She had a little bit of time. She would use that to give her horses baths before she needed to get them loaded to take in for the parade. She loved working with her Pasa Finos, not just because of their beauty and elegance, but because they had such sweet personalities. Of course, she was partial to any horse. She'd been horse crazy from the time she was little, and she was doing her dream job, living in her dream house, on her dream farm. Which was her family farm, the one that had been in her family for generations.

But sometimes people lived their dreams for a little while and then had to move on. Apparently that was what God was going to do with her, and she just had to accept it. There was no point in getting sad and falling into a deep depression because she wasn't getting what she wanted. After all, she needed to lift up her eyes and look for the door that God was going to open. She had convinced herself, almost anyway, that what God had planned for her was better than what she had. She just had to go through this rough patch first in order to get there.

Part of her didn't believe that, part of her wanted to think that God was actually out to get her and wanted to make her life as miserable as He possibly could. But most of her thought that she was right, that God was good, and in just a little while, she would see how very, very good He was.

Chapter Six

"I need to drop Larissa off at Summer's, so she can help Summer get ready for the parade," Gilbert's mother said as she bustled around the kitchen, tidying it up after lunch, since they were all planning on heading to the festival later.

"How about I do that?" Gilbert said, thinking that he wouldn't mind another chance to see the farm that he had put an offer on just a couple of hours ago. They hadn't even left the farm before they'd submitted it. He'd been right beside Jane as she typed it all up and had approved every word.

He knew that Summer was working and had plans to be in the parade, and she might not even look at the offer until that evening, so he wasn't completely disappointed that he hadn't heard anything from Jane.

But it wouldn't hurt for him to go, look at the farm again, and maybe put in a word for himself with Summer. He hadn't told his children, because since he had put in the offer, he figured he might as well wait. She had forty-eight hours to respond, and at this point, he might as well wait until she let him know. They'd waited this long. It wouldn't hurt them to not know at least until he found out for sure.

"Gram! I'm ready to go," Larissa said, popping into the kitchen with her hair in a ponytail and wearing a cute riding outfit.

He didn't even know she owned clothes like that. He supposed it made sense since he hadn't been taking his kids to the therapy sessions, he didn't know what they wore to them.

"I'm going to take you, kiddo. Is that okay?"

"Yeah! Maybe you can be in the parade too." Then her face fell. "Probably not. I've been working for weeks on the things I need to do in the parade. I don't think that you can just go in and be there without practicing."

"Yeah. Considering that I've never ridden a horse, I probably ought not to make my first ride in a parade, with people everywhere."

"Yeah," she said, jogging out the door and closing it behind her.

He figured that was his clue to go.

Before he reached the door, it opened again. He expected Larissa to come back through, having forgotten something. But it was Jones and Amy, his sister and brother-in-law.

"Hey, guys," he said, happy that they finally got together. Pretty much everyone in the world knew that they were perfect for each other, other than them, and they'd finally figured it out. He hadn't seen Amy look happier, and Jones looked pretty satisfied as well.

"Hey, I'm glad we caught you. I heard you made an offer on Summer's place."

"I did," he said, wondering how that had gotten out. The only people he had told were his mom and the realtor. He knew his mom hadn't told anyone. She was the kind of woman who always had cookies on the table, not the kind of woman who always had a phone to her ear spreading gossip.

"I guess someone had to. I know she's been struggling for a while, but I had hoped it wouldn't come to this." Amy looked truly sad.

"I think you're supposed to be happy for me because I'm buying a farm here in the area and I'm going to be moving close to all of you."

"Summer's been amazing with your kids. Do you know that she hasn't been charging you?"

Jones just stood back and let Amy talk, although Gilbert's eyes moved to him, and he nodded.

"I've heard that, and I appreciate it. I suppose I also tried to compensate her for it."

He had actually made his offer a little bit above the asking price. Not just so that he was sure to get the property, in case someone else was going to make an offer, sight unseen, but also because he knew that Summer had done that for him. He figured that extra little bit went a good ways toward compensating her for what she had done for him and his children. But that was his business, and he wasn't going to share that with his sister.

"I am happy for you. I'm sorry. I didn't mean to sound like I wasn't."

"We both are," Jones added. "Congratulations on putting an offer in. I hope you get it."

"Me, too. It's perfect for everything that I need. Not too big, but with plenty of room to grow, and we can have horses, which Larissa, especially, loves."

"She has really fallen in love with them, and she and Summer have a bond that...is pretty unique."

"Unique?" he asked, not sure if that was a good word or not. He didn't think that Summer had been taking advantage of Larissa, but he knew stranger things had happened, and with the way the world was today, he needed to be diligent in looking out for his kids.

"She just really got over Desire's death... I wouldn't say easily, but she just doesn't have any lasting effects from it. And I really think that Summer is the reason. And the horses too." Amy lifted her shoulder. "Animals just have a way of helping people, especially, but Summer really knew how to work everything out to the best advantage. She's a great counselor."

"Do you have to have a degree to do that?"

"I don't know if you have to, but I know Summer does. She talked about it a little bit. She went to the U of V."

"I see."

"So, I really hate seeing your children lose their excellent horse therapist. They've really come a long way under her guidance."

"Maybe wherever she goes, we can follow her." He hadn't really thought about that, but it seemed like a good idea. Especially since Amy was speaking of her so highly. "I'll make sure I tell her that I'd like to have her info once she knows where she's going. I can even ask her now if she has an idea. Maybe she does."

"I don't think she does. I know putting the farm up for sale was a hard step for her. It really tore at her heart because it had been in her family for so long, and it was the only home she's ever known."

"That's too bad. Sometimes life gives us hard knocks." No one could say that he hadn't been through those hard knocks. First his wife cheated, then she died, leaving him alone with three kids, and then his business almost went belly up. He knew a thing or two about hard knocks.

"That's true," Jones said, and Amy nodded. Amy and he had lost their dad at a young age, and before that, he hadn't been around much, so she knew a few things about hard knocks as well. And it seemed like Summer had led a charmed life up until now. So, he supposed it was her turn for the hard knocks, not that he didn't feel bad for her, because he did, it was just that everybody went through hard times. And there was nothing he could do about it.

Chapter Seven

"This is fun!" Larissa said as they walked their horses down the street, their flags streaming out behind them, waving to the crowd and occasionally throwing candy they had in their saddlebags.

"I always love parades," Summer said to Larissa, grateful that the little girl had been allowed to go. Her dad seemed kind of taciturn and stern. Losing his wife had probably taken a lot of the joy out of his life, and now he had three children he was trying to raise on his own. She supposed that would make anyone serious.

A band played ahead of them, and there were several fire trucks behind them, lights flashing, but no sirens. The crowd cheered occasionally for the twirlers who were right in front of them. One of them had lost her baton, and it ended up plinking down in front of Cricket, the horse Larissa rode.

Cricket didn't bat an eye. She was battle worn and tested and had been in more than her fair share of parades. No horse was bombproof, although Cricket was as close as they came. Summer would have been really upset if she had taken off down the street with Larissa on her back. There were times over the years where she'd had horses who had done exactly that to her. It was hard to get a horse used to crowds and noise without getting taken for a ride a time or two.

She wouldn't have trusted Larissa on Cricket if she hadn't been sure of her. Bunny was a little bit more skittish, but she was staying calm and doing fairly well.

Taking the horses in the parade was good for them, because it taught them to chill when it came to all the commotion around them.

She had gotten Gilbert's offer on the house when she'd run in to change her clothes after loading the horses on her trailer.

She hadn't responded to it, and she figured she could take a couple of hours to stew over it.

He'd offered her more than what she was asking.

Her realtor had been thrilled, and he'd counseled her to take it immediately.

The offer was good for forty-eight hours, but Summer figured she wouldn't make him wait that long. The thing was, he wanted to close in thirty days, and she would have to sell her horses, clean out her stuff, and find a place to live in less than a month. She wasn't sure she could do it. She hadn't been expecting the place to sell that fast, or maybe she just hadn't wanted it to.

"Hey, there's my dad and my brothers!" Larissa called, pointing over to a tall man standing with two young boys on either side of him. Lucas had grown since he first started coming to therapy, and he'd also gotten quieter. After his mother died, he barely said anything. It was currently her responsibility to try to help him work through his grieving. She thought they'd been doing rather well. He never would be the carefree boy he had been, but part of that was him growing up, and it wasn't just him losing his mother.

Robert, on the other hand, was back to being a typical nine-year-old. He grinned and waved and jumped when they threw extra candy in his direction.

Summer smiled, watching Robert jump all around for the candy, and Lucas, as mature as he tried to be, even scrambled for a few pieces of chocolate.

She looked away from the boys, and her eyes caught on Gilbert's. He was staring at her.

She smiled and waved, and tried not to let any of the turmoil in her heart show. This man would be living in her house. The house that her ancestors had grown up in, the house she had grown up in, the house that she had lived in her whole life. He would be making the decisions about it. Sitting in her kitchen, using her library, stabling his horses in her barn. Possibly getting married and bringing another wife home.

She looked away, telling herself that the kids she loved would be staying there as well. Robert and Lucas would grow up in her house, along with Larissa, who she loved and felt more affection toward than she did for any of her other students. It wasn't even close.

"They wanted to ride, but I told them they couldn't because they hadn't practiced."

"They're good enough riders that they probably could have, if I would have had enough horses." She felt the pang of losing Princess. It had been a huge blow to her business. Not just financially, but emotionally as well. Princess had been her go-to horse. Beautiful, regal, and super sweet. A baby could ride her and look good while she was doing it.

But Princess was gone, and she needed to move on. She couldn't keep regretting the fact that she had been lost. Although, she'd been over and over it already. Could she have done something different? She had been feeding everyone the same grass in the pasture. All the horses were out there. But for some reason, Princess was the only one who colicked.

Colic wasn't extremely well understood, and there were different kinds, but the basic gist of it was a horse couldn't burp, and if they had their feed changed too abruptly, or if they ate bad or moldy feed, or...some other things happened, it could send them into stomach cramps and intestinal agony that, without an operation, could kill a horse. Even with an operation, the horse could die, as Summer had found out. She already knew it; it just never happened to her before.

It seemed the parade was over in record time, and Miss Marjorie, Larissa's grandmother, was there to get her at the end of the parade route. Gilbert probably didn't know how lucky he was to have a mother like Miss Marjorie. He also had awesome sisters, and his children had been well taken care of while he had been off saving his business. Summer didn't know what she would have done if she had children. She had no parents to depend on and no siblings either. She felt like she was alone in the world, although she knew she had good friends.

She supposed she was going to have to talk to Sunny and see if Sunny would allow her to move in with her until she could figure out what she was going to do.

She walked both horses back to the trailer, took their tack off and put it in the appropriate compartments, watched as Larissa skipped off with her grandmother, then loaded both horses before driving home. She could have stayed and walked around the festival, but she wasn't feeling very festive. In fact, she was feeling downright morose. Totally normal for someone who was losing their home. Actually, she wasn't *losing* it. She was getting paid for it. It was going to be enough for her to pay everything off and have a little bit of money left over, and she needed to be happy about that.

As soon as she got home, she sat down at the bar in her beautiful, amazing kitchen, in the house she loved, and opened her laptop. Reading over the contract one last time, she took a deep breath, clicked the buttons to say that she agreed and to put her signature on the paper, and then hit send.

There. It was done. In thirty days, the farm would no longer be hers.

Chapter Eight

"**A**re you guys ready?" Gilbert asked as his kids hurried with their last-minute preparations.

"I'm ready," Larissa said, the overachiever of the group.

Even Lucas, with his silent stares and his mature actions, couldn't compare.

And Robert didn't even come close. "I'm still looking for my boots!" Robert called.

"The last time I saw them, they were on the back porch," his mother said from the kitchen where she was working on lunch. The kids would be hungry when they came back from their last ever horse therapy session.

Larissa, especially, was sad and gloomy, as much as she could be.

Gilbert had decided to take them himself. He was wrapping up loose ends at his business and had almost transitioned out of the office and completely to remote working. He would still pop in from time to time, but he could do it when the kids were at school.

"All right, I'm going to stay and keep an eye on the kids. I might as well watch them at least once and see what I've been missing all this time," he said. And he wanted to see the property that was going to be his on Tuesday of next week when he signed the papers.

He couldn't deny that he was excited. He was ready to make a fresh start, to have his children around him, and to become a family again. He thought the kids were ready for that too, although they were going to miss living with Grandma, which had been almost like a year-long vacation for them.

He supposed all of them would have some adjustments to make, including his mother. It was sad to lose the grandchildren she had grown to enjoy making noise around her house.

Of course, Isadora was still there with her three children, but they were much younger, and in Gilbert's opinion, younger children weren't as fun as his own children's age. In fact, so far, this was his favorite age. They were old enough to be fun but not so old that they were constantly challenging his authority or trying to do things that he didn't approve of. They still looked up to him and respected him, and honestly, they didn't give him much trouble at all.

He was grateful for that. Maybe the counseling had something to do with it, and he owed someone a huge thank you. Although, again, he kind of thought the fact that he offered her more than her asking price was a pretty big thank you.

He pulled into the farm, thinking that next week this time it would be his driveway and feeling a little thrill of excitement go through him.

The woman with the long blonde hair, Summer, was in the paddock, finishing up with an adult who was grooming a horse that was tied to the railing.

His mother had told him that the grooming of the horses was just as therapeutic as riding them had been. He knew that was true with Larissa. She loved making the horses look pretty. And he had to admit that Summer had gorgeous horses. Both of the horses she had in the parade were absolutely stunning, and he could tell that Larissa was proud to be riding. Although, as Gilbert watched, he found it was hard for him to take his eyes off the woman, and he didn't pay as much attention to the horse. He didn't understand why that was.

Maybe because she had her long blonde hair down, and it flowed in silky waves just like the mane of the horse. Or maybe it was because of the way she sat her horse, confident and sure, so much smaller than the animal under her, but totally in control.

Or maybe it was her smile, despite the fact that he knew that she was facing sorrow and hardship. He admired bravery and self-control, and Summer showed both.

Whatever it was, he felt his eyes drawn to her again, when he would rather have been looking over the property that would soon be his.

"She's brushing Cricket!" Larissa said. "That's the horse I usually ride."

"I wonder where Bunny is? That's my horse," Robert said.

"She's probably in the barn. She said not too many people ride her." Lucas spoke up from the passenger seat. His eyes were glowing, and he looked more alive than he had the entire week at school.

Maybe this horse therapy thing really was beneficial.

Of course, he knew it was. He'd seen the results with his own eyes, and even if he hadn't, his mother and sisters gushed over it. Even Jones and Judd, his brothers-in-law, spoke up in defense of how good it was for the kids.

He parked at the front of the stable, noting the flowers that grew there and remembering the plants that had been in the kitchen. Apparently, Summer enjoyed growing things. He appreciated the burst of color, even though it was almost the middle of November.

Usually they had a frost at this elevation long before now, but after a cool, dry summer, they'd been having a prolonged warm spell this fall.

"We're buying your farm!" Larissa said as she jumped out of the car and started going to Summer who had come out to greet them.

To Summer's credit, she smiled, and even looked happy for

Larissa, as she nodded and said, "I know. Next week, this will be yours."

Her eyes flitted to Gilbert's, and Gilbert felt a guilty flush staining his cheeks. He didn't mean for it to. He had no idea why he would feel guilty. He hadn't done anything wrong. He'd done this woman a favor. Her farm had been purchased for more than she was asking for it, and she should be thanking him.

He didn't know why he was so defensive. She hadn't said a word and just looked happy for Larissa.

"Are you going to leave the horses here? Are they going to be our horses now?" Robert asked as he ran over to Summer, throwing his arms around her waist.

Summer didn't hesitate but hugged him back. He supposed that was a difference between counseling children and counseling adults. A counselor could never hug a client, but sometimes human beings just needed that reassuring touch, that comfort that only the touch and arms of another human could give.

With children, it was a little different. Especially with a woman counseling them. Affection flowed freely between the three of his children and Summer.

"I don't think so. I'm looking to sell them, and I think I have at least three of them sold. So, no to that."

"Which three?" Lucas asked, his brows furrowing, as though the idea bothered him. Gilbert had closed his door and stood a little bit away, allowing the children to interact freely without him interfering. He had meant to come, stand back and watch, not get involved. He was curious to see exactly what all Summer did when she worked with the kids, since everyone talked about her and praised her so highly.

"Thatcher is one," she said gently, and Gilbert remembered Lucas saying that Thatcher was the horse he often road.

His face fell.

"He's going to a really good home. It's not another therapy stable, but it's a riding stable, where he'll get to go on trail rides with other kids and their families. I'm sure he's going to love it there."

"But I'm gonna miss him," Lucas said, and he sounded a little bit belligerent. Like he was trying to be tough and hide the fact that the news had shocked and saddened him. Maybe he was even thinking about crying.

Gilbert hadn't considered making an offer on the horses while he had been there looking at the farm. He should have considered it, and he wished he would have known she was going to sell them.

"What about Cricket? Are you selling her?"

"Yes, Cricket is an awesome horse, and it was easy for me to find a buyer for her. She's going to the farm of a friend of mine. We've been good friends for a long time, and she also has a stable full of horses, and she gives riding lessons. So Cricket and Bunny are both going there. Their students are going to love getting to take lessons on such beautiful horses."

"That stinks," Larissa said. "How far away is it?"

"It's about three hours from here."

"Three hours? We'll never see them again." Then she turned to Gilbert. "Daddy? Can we go visit Cricket and Bunny?"

"And Thatcher," Lucas said.

"I don't see why not. Maybe next summer when we have plenty of time where we can take a day to drive."

The kids talked a bit more, and then Summer sent them in to start brushing their mounts.

"Thanks for bringing them," she said, looking up, her body partially turning like she was getting ready to walk away.

"I was going to stay and watch if that's okay."

"Sure. That's fine. You can walk through the stable, or you can just hang out there on the railing. You'll be able to see everything from there once we get the horses out and start riding."

"All right. I wish I would have known or thought to ask what you are going to do with the horses. I probably couldn't afford to buy all of them, but the kids seem pretty attached to them."

"They do. And I actually sold them for much less than what they're worth in order for them to be able to go to good homes. I... I appreciate your offer being more than the asking price, and it enabled me to be a little bit more choosy about the home for my horses." She paused. "Thank you."

"My pleasure. I understand that you've been giving my children counseling sessions without charging for them. I felt like it was the least I could do."

"Your children are special. I felt especially bad for them because they had the double whammy of losing their mom and having you go and spend time with the business to keep it from going under." She paused and then added softly, "I hope that doesn't sound like I was prying. It's just comments that your sisters and mother have made while they've been here."

"No problem. That's common knowledge, and I wouldn't have thought that you were prying. I understand from them that you care a lot about the children, and I see a big difference in them. My family credits a lot of that to you."

She gave a small smile, and nodded her head, but didn't agree or disagree. "They've done excellent. I've been very pleased with their progress. They all had great attitudes, although the first few months this year, January and February, were a little bit tough. Not only because we couldn't always get out in the ring and ride, but because I know they were dealing with a lot, losing their mom and making all those adjustments."

"Yeah. It was a tough year for all of us, but the future looks bright, and I definitely fell in love with your property. It's beautiful."

"Yeah. I've been blessed, and I'm grateful that it'll have children on it again. And children I love. I don't say this very often, but of all of my clients, they're my favorites."

Maybe that explained why she had given them therapy for free. Or maybe she was just generous with all of her clients that way. If so, it was no wonder that she lost her farm. He hated to think like that, since generosity shouldn't be punished by the loss of one's livelihood, but on the other hand, a person couldn't have a business and not charge, or they would go out of business rather quickly, as he was pretty sure Summer could testify to.

"Do you have a place to stay?" he asked, and he wasn't sure why the question came out of his mouth.

"Yeah. I got a room with a friend in Mistletoe Meadows. So I won't be far away."

"But if you're getting rid of all of your horses, you won't be giving therapy lessons anymore." He knew that. After all, they'd made a big deal about this being the last day for his kids for therapy. So, most likely everyone she had been giving lessons to were having their last days for the last two weeks or so.

"No. I'm going to have to do something else. Whether it's going to be opening up a regular therapy practice or something along those lines, I don't know. I've always loved working with horses, and I've never lived anywhere but the farm, so it's going to be a little bit of an adjustment for me, but you made it through this year and your big adjustment, so I'm sure I'm going to make it through the next year and my adjustments as well."

She put on a brave smile, and then she lifted a hand. "I need to go in with the kids. You're welcome to hang around wherever you want. And if you're up to it, we can get a horse out and you can have a horse of your own to work with. Although, we might not have you riding today."

"I've never ridden before, so I'll probably take a little bit of extra instruction before I'm able to get up on the back of a horse, so I think I'll just watch from the side for today." He almost said maybe next time he'd try riding, but then he remembered that there wasn't going to be a next time.

She smiled, and he thought he saw sadness in her eyes, but her smile was genuine, and she seemed friendly and not bitter or angry at all. Like she'd accepted the fact that God had taken something away from her, and she was just waiting for Him to show her what He was going to give her as a replacement.

Interesting, since Gilbert had never thought about God replacing his wife. In fact, he hadn't thought about getting married again at all. He had to admit finding out that his wife had cheated, and then going through the cancer, the treatments, the bad news after bad news, and seeing his children heartbroken as they lost their mother, had left a mark on him.

He hadn't been heartbroken as much as he'd been…devastated because of his kids, and concerned about his business, and alone as a single dad, rather unsure of what to do, since he'd never parented without his wife, obviously.

Regardless, he got through it, and she would too.

Chapter Nine

Gilbert stood the whole time at the fence, watching. Summer often had parents watch their children's sessions, and sometimes adults brought friends or relatives or even siblings or kids to watch their sessions as well. In fact, more often than not she had someone standing at the rail watching her. And she long ago ceased to be nervous about it.

She didn't know why she was very conscious of Gilbert's eyes on the back of her head at this point. She should be immune to that by now, but she found she wasn't.

"Good job, Larissa. Cricket is really paying attention to you. Your feet are in the correct position, and you only need to straighten your back just a bit," she called out to Larissa.

Larissa straightened her back, not realizing she'd been slouching, and continued around the ring. Lucas rode with authority on Thatcher. Thatcher was a great horse, always willing and very careful of whatever load he held. He had been great for Lucas. And she felt like Lucas and Thatcher had bonded. She very seldom had to remind Lucas of anything that he needed to do, and Lucas was always very conscientious and considerate of Thatcher after they were done.

"Good job, Robert. Keep your feet out," she reminded him as he came around, a big smile on his face. She returned the smile and noted that he obeyed immediately, his feet pointing in the proper direction as he passed her.

It was time for the kids to get off, but she was loathe to end their session. She didn't have anyone else coming; this was her very last therapy session ever. At least on this farm, with these horses.

She'd almost not gotten through her conversation with Gilbert without crying. She'd fallen in love with each of these horses, and it was going to kill her to see them go in all different directions, but she was serious when she said that they were going to good homes. She really had knocked the price down way below what they were actually worth so that she could sell them before she moved and to good homes, where she knew they would be taken care of. So often, people who didn't know anything about horses bought them, thinking it would be easy, not realizing that they needed regular farrier care, vaccinations, grooming, their stalls cleaned out on a daily basis, and good, fresh, mold-free hay to eat, which was not cheap.

Often those horses got dumped off at an auction, since the same people who had bought them had no clue on how or where to sell them.

It was just a fact of life, but if she could help it, it wasn't going to happen to the horses who had served her for years and helped her build her business. It would have been a roaring success if she hadn't inherited so much debt from her parents.

Regardless, she wasn't going to think about the what-ifs. She was going to get through this hard part and wait for God to open up His windows of blessing on her. She knew they were going to open, and at any time.

She just didn't know how or when, and it might not be exactly what she wanted, but she knew it would be exactly what she needed. God was so good that way. He never gave her something she didn't need. He always had her edification in mind.

"All right, guys. Let's dismount, and we'll untack the horses and brush them out."

It was her favorite part. She loved riding, always had, but with the horses that she had, there wasn't anything she loved better than brushing them and making them look beautiful. Their manes and tails were so long and flowing, she would never get tired of looking at them. The way they moved, the way they held their heads, the fluid grace that they had, combined with their beautiful hair and coloring, was enough to make her content to just sit and look at them all day long.

Not that she ever had that kind of time, but she would if she could.

She tried not to think about how this was her last session, her last call to dismount, her last time to watch the children brush out the manes and tails and give Thatcher and Bunny and Cricket all the attention they could, since they would be leaving over the weekend.

"Where are you going?" Robert asked once they had their horses tied up and had started brushing them.

"Today?" she asked, wondering why he wanted to know what her plans were for the day.

"No. Dad said we were going to move here, and I want to know where you're going?"

"Oh. Right now, I'm going to be moving in with a friend in town, but... I won't be staying there forever."

"Why don't you just stay here with us? You could live here. I would share my bedroom with you. Daddy said I was going to get my own all to myself."

"Well, that's very nice of you, Larissa. I appreciate that. But I think you and your daddy and your brothers need a place of your own without me interfering. Plus, if it's not mine anymore, it's kind of silly for me to stay here."

"But I want you here. It won't be the same without you. And if the horses aren't in the stalls, and they're not here to ride, it's not going to be the same at all." Lucas made an impassioned plea, which was rather out of character. Especially as he'd gotten quieter and quieter.

"I'm going to be fine, and so are you. Maybe your dad will get you horses, and you'll have new horses to stay in the stalls and to ride. And if you're here and the horses are yours, you might be able to ride on the pasture field, which you were never able to do with me. Think about how much fun that will be."

She tried to make it sound like it would be exciting and fun. She didn't want the kids to be sad. The whole point of her therapy sessions was to try to help them work through that, so that they could look forward to all the happy things that were going to be happening in their lives, and realize that they had the ability to take control of their emotions, and not feel like they were tossed and turned by every little thing that happened.

That was one of the problems the children had. There was so much that they didn't control, not just with death and suffering, but having to go to school and following their parents' rules, which was very good, but being in charge of their own horse, riding it, brushing it, gave them the chance to be strong, be the one who was in charge, and realize that they could depend on themselves for certain things and that they weren't completely powerless. It gave them power that they weren't used to and showed them that they were quite capable.

She thought it had worked well with the children, but she was disappointed she wouldn't be around to see them grow up and to see the adults they would become. If things had gone well, she would have stayed in Mistletoe Meadows until she died, but it probably wasn't a big enough town for her to be able to open a regular counseling practice. She needed to go to someplace a little bigger. Like Harrisonburg.

At last, forty-five minutes after their therapy session was supposed to be over, she finally said, "All right, guys, it's time for us to pack it up."

"I don't want to leave," Larissa said, sniffing and holding onto Cricket's neck. "I may never see Cricket again."

"We'll make sure to visit her, honey." Gilbert's voice came from behind them.

Summer had been so aware of him when they were out riding in the ring, but she'd kind of forgotten about him as she watched the children take care of the horses, thinking about how far they'd come and how much the therapy had helped them and how much she was going to miss them.

The kids all protested, even Lucas, who didn't want to leave Thatcher.

It broke Summer's heart to see the children so unhappy. And she wondered if all of the work that they had done in therapy was going to be undone. They'd gotten over their mother's passing, and they'd been taught self-reliance, patience, and a work ethic that included thinking of others before they thought of themselves, since of course, a horse person always had to take care of their horse first.

But maybe all of that would be lost in their grief over being separated from their beloved horses.

Still, in another five minutes or so, they had gotten in the car, with Gilbert giving her one last thoughtful look before he got in and drove away.

That's when Summer finally allowed her own tears to fall, holding onto Cricket's mane and crying softly. Everything she had ever known was being taken from her.

No. She was voluntarily selling everything she knew so that she could start another life, wherever God wanted her. She had to think about it like that. She couldn't think about it any other way, or she wasn't sure she would be able to function.

Chapter Ten

"Congratulations, you just bought yourself a house," Jane said as she held the key across the table and dangled it in front of Gilbert.

Gilbert slowly held his hand out, and the key, cold and hard, dropped into it.

This was Summer's key. The woman his children loved, who had done so much for them with her horses and her generous spirit and the love and patience and kindness that she had shown to them.

He hadn't really grasped it until he had seen her at work. She was loving and patient but also encouraged and exhorted his children to do better, to be better, to think for themselves, to have confidence in their ability. He saw now why his mother and sisters had raved about her. She was most definitely the reason that his children were doing so well. Except, in the last few days, since they'd said goodbye, his kids had been quiet and subdued, and if he had to use a word to describe them, he would use depressed. They seemed like they were depressed.

Unfortunately, he wasn't sure what to do about it. She said she'd already sold her horses, and she had plans to move somewhere else, and it wasn't like he could...do what? Buy her horses back? He didn't have the money for that. And it wasn't like he could offer to live somewhere else so she could stay on the farm. He couldn't do that either.

He didn't see any solutions, and honestly, he thought that maybe this was just one of those hard things people had to get through.

It was easier to do when someone had a therapist like Summer, but what Summer had taught his children should serve them well now. Plus, school was gearing up, and they had activities that should be taking their attention. Like the Thanksgiving parade that was happening at the end of next week.

Except, the idea of a parade had made Larissa cry when she'd asked if she would be able to ride a horse in it, and he reminded her that Summer had sold her horses, and Summer wasn't on the farm anymore.

Yeah, that had gone over well. Not.

"Thanks a lot," he told Jane, looking at the key in his hand.

"I talked to Frederick, Summer's realtor, and he said that the house was empty, anything that was left was yours to do whatever you wanted to with, and Summer planned to be gone from the premises last night. So, it's all yours, and you can move in whatever you want."

"Sounds good. It was nice doing business with you."

"It was wonderful to do business with you as well. If you're ever in the market for real estate, please keep me in mind," Jane said, and Gilbert figured that she probably was pretty happy, since she made a nice, tidy sum and all she'd had to do was show the house one time.

He walked out of the real estate office, strangely sad rather than jubilant that he'd been able to turn his business around, along with his life, and provide a farm and place to live with his children. A new beginning if one would.

Instead, he thought about Summer, the horses, and how depressed his children had been. And wished that there had been a way to save all of that. It seemed sad that someone who had done so much good had lost everything.

He tried to remind himself that she had the money from the sale of the farm, and it wasn't like she was destitute. She would land on her feet and do something else, just as he had when his wife died. Sometimes a person just had to carry on, even though they didn't want to.

He drove home, trying to think about the excitement of moving into a new home and not about the status of the prior owner. Somehow, when he had sold the house that he and Desire had lived in together, it hadn't been nearly this hard.

He walked in. All the kids sat at the table with his mother, schoolbooks open, or in Robert's case, he sat with a reading book in his hand.

"How do you guys feel about going to see our new house?"

"Yay!" Larissa said, jumping up. "Maybe she left the horses there after all!" She grinned. "Maybe Miss Summer will be hiding upstairs in the loft."

That reminded Gilbert that there was a loft apartment above the stables. He'd never gone out to see it.

He had already been sold on the place and hadn't needed to. Maybe he'd go up and check it out, although he highly doubted that Summer would be hiding in it.

"All right, let's go. Mom, if you want to come along and check it out, you can."

"How about I drive separately, because I might not want to stay as long as you guys do."

"That's just fine. Come anytime. You're welcome to our new home. I have to get a duplicate key made." He held up the key that dangled from his hand. He hadn't noticed when Jane had handed it to him, but it was on a keychain with a horse attached to it as a little charm.

It was cute and suited someone who had done horse therapy for a living.

It didn't take long to get the kids in the car and drive to their new farm.

Somehow it wasn't quite as victorious a feeling as he had thought it would be to pull into the drive. Their own farm, but the kids were strangely silent as they pulled into the house.

"I came in here once to go to the bathroom," Larissa said softly.

"I thought there was a bathroom in the barn?"

"We went in and got a drink too. We didn't stay in long, but her kitchen was really nice. She had plants in it, and Grandma would like it."

"I thought so too when I saw it," he said, trying to force some happiness into his voice.

As they walked around the house, his mom really did ooh and aah over the kitchen, but the plants were gone. The library still held some books, but most of those were gone as well. All of the little touches that he had noticed when he had gone through had disappeared, even the beds were stripped of the bedding, although the beds themselves were still there. He wondered if she hadn't been able to afford to hire movers to move the beds, but more likely, she didn't have any place to put them, unless she wanted to rent a storage unit, which he would bet that she didn't want to pay the expense. Plus, what would a single woman with no children need with six beds?

She hadn't mentioned that she was going to leave them, but he should thank her, because now he didn't have to buy them.

He just needed to procure bedding.

"Are you okay?" His mom had come up to him, and he hadn't even heard her. He tried not to startle too badly.

"Yeah. Why?" Vaguely he was aware that his children ran around trying to figure out which bedrooms they wanted, although Lucas seemed almost as disinterested as he did.

Lucas was the one who struggled most with the loss of his horse, which was somewhat surprising considering how much Larissa had loved hers.

"I know. You just seem…sad. Are you thinking about Desire?"

"No. Not at all." It had been a while since he had thought about her with anything other than a passing question in his mind as to whether or not he would have been divorced at this time if she were still alive and hadn't had cancer. He didn't really miss her. They had not exactly reconciled but had managed to find a truce, but then she'd been diagnosed, and he wasn't sure whether she would keep her word. After all, she'd broken it once already.

"All right. I just think this would be a happier time, and you almost seem… I don't know, like you're not really happy that you guys finally have a house together. You know you don't have to move out if you don't want to," she said, and he wanted to reassure her that it was perfectly fine, although maybe if she had said that a month ago, he might have decided to stay.

No, a month ago he was determined to buy this farm, but now, he almost wondered if it might have been wiser for him to somehow help Summer keep it, rather than thinking he was helping her by buying it.

It was too late.

"No. I'm excited. I'm happy there's beds here because we can sleep here tonight if we want to."

"You know you're still welcome for Sunday lunch," his mom said with a smile.

"I know. We'll be there after church for sure."

"And don't forget, Terry and Judd usually take your kids in, so they'll need to pick them up here. You're going to need to let them know that they need to stop by with the horse and wagon."

"Are they doing that again already?"

"They are. They would have started last week, but one of the horses needed a shoe."

"I see. I'll text him right now." He pulled his phone out while his mom said, "I'm going to head out. I know Isadora's children are going to be going down for naps soon, and I usually try to give her a hand."

"All right. You know you're welcome to come here anytime you want to to get away from all the noise and hubbub if you need to. And to use my awesome kitchen."

His mom smiled and looked around once more as they reached the bottom of the stairs. "It's a beautiful house. And the kitchen really is awesome. Larissa is going to enjoy it."

"I know she will. And if you hear that anyone has any horses for sale, I'm in the market for a couple of good, calm horses for the kids."

"I'll keep an ear out," his mom said, then she waved and headed out the door.

He felt strangely lonely after she left. The house was so big, and... He hadn't really felt alone, not even after Desire died. He'd always been with his family, his sisters and their husbands coming in and out at his mom's house, as well as his brothers, and there was just always something going on. Of course, he was spending so much time rebuilding his business too, and now... He felt lonely.

"Can I have the bedroom with the blue walls?" Robert asked as he came running downstairs.

"You sure can," he said. "As long as no one else wants it. If someone else does, we'll have to flip for it or something."

"We're all going to get different rooms. So, are we allowed to pick what we want?"

"Yeah. I want the one at the end of the hall. Is that one open?"

"Why do you want one? It doesn't have a bathroom with it?" Lucas asked Robert.

"If you have a room with a bathroom, you know you're going to have to clean it, right?"

"Okay. I know how to clean bathrooms. Grandma taught me."

Another thing he should thank his mom for. He nodded, and then the kids went tearing back upstairs. He was going to have to go to the store and grab linens, and he probably ought to try to figure out what size the beds were. But first, he wandered into the kitchen.

It looked a lot more dreary without the plants. Maybe he'd have to try to find some, although he'd never been very good at keeping anything alive. Not like Summer obviously was. Maybe he could ask her what kind of plants grew well there, but... Where would he ever find her to ask?

Lord? Did I get ahead of You somehow? Is this really what I was supposed to do?

He knew now was not the time to start questioning it. He should have asked for God's direction back when he was buying the farm, but he'd been so sure everything was falling into place that it hadn't really occurred to him to check and make sure that God was in it.

Not that he would have been able to tell if He wasn't. It just seemed so perfect, it almost had to come from the Lord.

The feeling would pass, and he would settle down and be content here, as would his children. He was sure of it.

Chapter Eleven

"Thanks so much for letting me work here. I am not sure what to do, and it's nice to just have a place to stay. I promise I'm not going to be here forever." Summer spoke to Sunny, who had agreed to allow her to work in her bakeshop and live above it for a time, until she could figure out what to do.

"I'm always looking for good, reliable help. And someone who lives in my place where I can beat the door down and yank her out of bed if she's late for work is my idea of an ideal employee," Sunny said with a grin.

Summer laughed. One of the benefits of living with Sunny was she got to listen to her practice, which she had done the last two nights. Today, Monday morning, she started her new job at the bakery. She wasn't cooking anything, thankfully, since she was a terrible cook, but she was responsible for running the cash register and making sure that the display case stayed stocked, as well as filling orders as they came in, either online or over the phone.

It wouldn't be too hard. There were a few tables where people could sit and enjoy the goodies that they had bought, and she was responsible for keeping them cleaned and wiped as well.

Nothing difficult, nothing that would be taxing for her brain, and it would give her plenty of time to think.

Not that that was necessarily a good thing, but at least she didn't worry about messing anything up. And she had a soft place to land until she figured out what she was going to do next. She had sent her resume to a few places that were looking for a therapist to add to their practice, and she had scheduled several appointments to go and look at office space in Harrisonburg.

Maybe none of that stuff would pan out, and she almost hoped it didn't. She wanted to have a job that dealt with horses, except the idea of working with horses was almost heartbreaking, when she thought about Bunny and Cricket and Thatcher all going to different places, and that the horses that she worked with would be different.

But that was life. Animals came and went, and she had to be okay with that.

The morning passed uneventfully, until around 11 AM when she had just finished scribbling down an order on the notepad, hung up the phone, and checked the display case to see that it was full when she looked up and saw Gilbert McBride standing in front of her.

They stared at each other for a little bit before she got her wits about her.

"Good morning." Thankfully her voice didn't sound too perky or fake. But it had enough warmth and welcoming that she felt like she was doing a good job. "Can I help you?"

"Summer. I wasn't expecting to see you here."

It was obvious that she had flummoxed him. She didn't know why. It wasn't like seeing her should bring any kind of shock to him. She hadn't done anything unkind to him and in fact had left a lot of the things that she couldn't take with her at the farm for him to use, hoping it would help him out.

"Well, I'm here. And I will be for a little bit. I hope you're enjoying the farm. I didn't mention it, but I left the beds, because I figured you'd have more use for them than I did."

"I appreciate it. We...enjoy it there."

"Good. It's a great place for kids to grow up."

He nodded. "It is."

There was an awkward silence, and then she said, "So, can I get you something?" She thought she'd already asked him, but she couldn't remember for sure. She needed to make sure she was doing her job here.

"Um, uh, oh, yeah." Obviously he was having trouble finding his words. She waited patiently. She hadn't meant to upset him with her presence, but there wasn't anything she could do to fix it. Other than trying not to make him any more embarrassed than what he already was.

"I'll take a blueberry muffin. And coffee. Black."

She nodded and smiled. "Coming right up."

She got him a muffin, set it on the counter, and poured him a cup of black coffee. She rang it up, and he paid with a card. As she handed him the receipt back and he signed it, he said, "I'm looking for some horses if you know anyone who's selling them."

"I'll keep that in mind. Do you have a price range?"

"They can't be too expensive. I spent all my money on this farm that I just bought."

She laughed. "It's a nice farm. I think that investment will be worth it in the long run."

She hoped he felt that way; she sure did. If she were going to be raising children, that would be the place she would want to do it.

"I think so too."

She smiled, and he turned around and took one step before he turned back around.

She got caught watching him walk away. He was tall, handsome, maybe with a few gray hairs in his temple, but that only made him look more distinguished, as gray hair often did on men. His blue eyes were kind, and his strong nose and jaw might have been a little bit too bold for him to be considered handsome, but she thought them striking.

That, along with the broad shoulders and confident demeanor, caught her eye, and she wondered that she never noticed any of it before.

Of course, he was the man who'd bought her farm, the father of her therapy students, not someone she was interested in romantically. This was the absolute worst time of her life to get involved with someone, and she definitely didn't want to be involved with someone who lived in her old house. It would be too...painful when they broke up. And... Where was she going with that?

She shook her head and tilted it. "Did you forget something?"

"So... Are you done with therapy?" He cleared his throat and lifted a hand, holding it out. "Sorry. Don't mean to pry. You were just so good with the kids. And honestly they've been struggling getting over not seeing you, not seeing the horses, and all that, and it just seems like a shame that you're not doing that anymore when you're so good at it."

"Well, it's not like you can do horse therapy from just anywhere. You kinda have to have a place to keep your horses, and since I don't anymore, unless I find something, which I haven't so far, I'll be just doing regular therapy."

"Here in Mistletoe Meadows?" he asked.

"I'm looking at a few places in Harrisonburg and even further north in Winchester. We'll see what the Lord has for me. I'm sure there's something He's just waiting for me to have. He's got something for me."

"I'm sure He does. He really used you, in my family anyway."

"Thank you. Your children are special to me." That was the truth.

He turned away, and then she deliberately looked down. She would not watch him walk away again. So, she was surprised when he set his muffin down on the counter.

He leaned forward and said, "Are you happy doing this?"

"This?" she asked, looking around and assuming that he meant working the cash register here at the bakery.

"Yeah. This job. This is really what you want?"

"No, but you don't always get what you want. Didn't we just say that?" Now he was being weird. But it was interesting. She wasn't put off by it, she almost felt like he…cared.

She shoved whatever odd feelings were welling up in her chest aside and gave him a curious look.

"I'm sorry. I'm acting oddly, because I just had an idea, and I'm not sure how to approach it with you. It's a little off-the-wall."

"All right."

"So… Okay, I know you already sold your horses, but there's that apartment above the stables. And you would be welcome to stay there if you wanted to. I don't know if you can get your horses back, but if you could, you could keep them in the stable. And there's plenty of bedrooms in the house." He held up a hand. "I know that's a little bit…funny, but I don't mean anything by it. I'm just saying there's plenty of room on the farm for you to live there, too. I can't shake the bad feeling that I've had ever since I moved in. Can't shake the way the kids felt when they were with you, how you help them, how generous you were with my family, how you helped my kids through one of the hardest times of their lives, and here you are in a hard time, and I kind of thought I was helping you by offering you more for your farm than what it was worth, but I think I could have helped you more by…figuring out how to help you keep it."

She blinked, and her mind started whirling as soon as he said he didn't know whether she could get her horses back or not.

She knew for a fact she could. Everyone that she sold them to— they were all friends who knew her circumstances—would sell them back for exactly the amount they paid for them, and she still had that money. She hadn't needed to sell her horses because of the amount that he had paid for the farm. She just hadn't had a place to keep them. And she knew she could get them all back. But… Was this God opening a door or was this just Him tempting her with something she really wanted, and she should decline and wait for the thing He really wanted to give her?

"That's...very generous of you. I wouldn't want to put your family out though."

"You wouldn't. I mean, I guess we'd have to figure out how to split the barn, since you would need it for your job, and... You didn't charge my family for therapy for the last year. I wouldn't charge you for the use of the barn. That seems fair to me, but... I know my kids would want to be able to use the barn and have horses that they could ride, and I know that you wouldn't be able to have them around while you were doing therapy, if you could even get your clients back." He lifted a hand and shrugged his shoulders. "I'm sorry, I'm kind of rambling, but I'm thinking out loud. I just...would love to see you be able to continue to do what you love and are good at, and somehow fit the kids and me in around it."

"I love this idea. But how about you let me think about it and pray about it, and you do the same thing, and... Maybe we can talk about it in a day or two and see how you feel?"

"Yeah. I think that's a good idea. You pray about it, I will too, and we'll see what we come up with. I can come back in here for another muffin. Now that I know you work here. Will you be working on Wednesday?"

"Yeah. I will. I'll actually be here all day, because the parade is Wednesday night."

He nodded absently. Apparently he had forgotten about the parade. But it didn't matter. Not to her. She wasn't riding in it, she was working through it, and Sunny expected to be extremely busy that evening. Sunny would be in the parade, playing the cello, so it was going to be up to Summer to hold down the fort, so to speak.

"All right then. I'll see you Wednesday." He nodded at her, and started away, then turned back around, setting his muffin down one last time. "I thought I probably ought to give you my phone number. If you have any questions, or ideas, or things that you think I need to think about before we talk about it, just give me a call or text me, okay?"

"Sure," she said, unable to contain her smile that he kept walking away and coming back, although this time, he seemed a lot more like his normal, competent self.

And to think she thought he was a jerk. He didn't seem like that at all, he just had a serious demeanor that belied a soft heart. There were very few people she knew who would buy a home and then open it up to an almost stranger, just because he felt compassion for them. She refused to label it pity. She could stand on her own two feet, but sometimes God didn't want a person to do that. Sometimes God wanted a person to accept outside help and to work with other people in order to accomplish the things that needed to be done.

He gave her his number, and she hesitated a moment before she texted "hi."

"That way you have mine too," she said, thinking that she was probably safe giving him her number. After all, this was Marjorie's son, and Marjorie was one of the sweetest, most godly women she knew. In fact, if she could choose her mother, she would have chosen Marjorie.

"All right. It's settled. Text me if you need me, I'll do the same, and I'll see you on Wednesday."

"We'll be busy in the evening, so I might not have a whole lot of time to talk."

"I'll keep that in mind. Maybe I'll wait until the crowd leaves, and we can chat, if you don't think you'll be too tired."

"No. I don't think I'll be too tired." She would make sure she wasn't too tired, because somehow in her heart, she started getting excited about being able to move back to her farm. The problem was, she would have to stop thinking about it as her farm. And how long would it last? How long would he allow her to work on his property, running her business from his barn? What if he got upset? Could he just kick her out of his house?

She wasn't sure the apartment over the stable was livable. The last she remembered, there wasn't even a bed in it. It was the one place on the farm that could use a substantial upgrade.

But if it got her back on the property, that would be good.

Maybe she shouldn't worry about the future. Maybe she shouldn't be concerned about how things would work out down the road. Maybe it was up to the Lord to work all that out, and she just had to step through the door He opened.

Although, on the other hand, she felt like it would be wise to think things through and make sure that she was making a wise decision. She should have safeguards in place for herself.

Of course, man's wisdom wasn't always God's wisdom, and she needed to remember that.

"Who is that? Did he just give you his number?" Sunny came out of the back, and from the look on her face, Summer assumed that she'd been watching for quite a while.

"It's the dude who bought the farm," Summer said quietly, almost thoughtfully. The whole exchange seemed strange and left her with this odd feeling. This...strange desire to go running after him.

She didn't quite get that, but she shook it off.

"Wow. So why did you give him your number?"

"Actually, he gave me his. He...invited me to live on the farm and start my equine therapy business back up again."

"But you sold your horses," Sunny said, setting the tray of muffins that she'd brought out from the back down and carefully putting them into the display case.

"I know. I know I could buy them all back, but... It would be weird, working with him, not owning the farm, I mean...would he kick me off anytime he wanted to?"

"That's something you'd have to figure out. You have to have some kind of agreement in place and whatever rent he was going to charge you."

She hesitated, and then she said, "He wasn't going to charge me anything, because I've been giving his kids free therapy since before his wife died."

She didn't want to brag about that. She didn't do it for the accolades or to have anyone think she was a good person. She just did it because...she felt like they needed it, and she heard that his business was on the brink, so she wanted to do what she could to help.

She'd never refused anyone because they couldn't pay. Although, she knew she had to run a business, and in order to do that, she had to make enough money to pay her bills.

So it wasn't like she went around handing out free stuff all the time.

"Wow. I didn't know that. So he's not going to charge you?"

"No. But like you said, we still have to have some kind of agreement in place. If I am running a business out of there, he can't just kick me out."

"I don't have any guarantees that I'm going to be able to renew my lease every year. They could just decide they want to sell the building and I'm out of the place to work. So, that wouldn't be too much different than what I've got here."

"All right. I guess... I've always worked on my own farm, and I didn't really realize how those things work."

"Typically you sign the lease, it could be six months or a year. I suppose there are longer leases, although I've never had one. But there's no guarantee that you'll get offered another six months or a year. And they can raise your monthly payment anytime they want to."

"That hardly seems fair."

"I know, right?"

"Yeah. Maybe this is a better offer than I thought."

"I guess I just wouldn't worry about whether or not he's going to rip the rug out from underneath you. Doing equine therapy is what you were born for. You're so good at it, and everyone says that, not that I want to lose the best worker I've ever had."

"This is my first day."

"I know. And this says something about the quality of workers I've had." They laughed together.

"Well, I guess if you think it's a good idea, that kinda sways my opinion a bit, because I was concerned about getting into something where I might end up getting the short end of the stick."

"It's totally up to you, of course, but I guess I wouldn't let that bother me if I were you. After all, it could happen anywhere, not just with him. Although, with your horses it would be nice to have a little bit of advance notice, but maybe you could put that in the lease, that you needed a month's notice if he's going to sell the farm or not allow you to stay anymore."

"Yeah. That's smart. I suppose I ought to see a lawyer."

"You could probably download something from online. I know a lawyer would be recommended, but I tend to avoid them."

"Same. But I guess I have another question if you've got some time."

"I sure do. This is kind of exciting, although I'm not trying to get rid of you. You're welcome to stay. I was looking forward to having a roommate and friend."

"And I was looking forward to staying and having a change of pace, although the idea of getting my horses back and hopefully getting most of my clients back really has me excited."

It was also exciting for her to be in contact with Gilbert some more. He...had some kind of aura around him that drew her. She wasn't sure what it was. But she remembered how nervous she was when he had been watching her. She hadn't really thought about it too much then, other than it was strange, but... She noticed him in a way she didn't normally notice people.

"I'm sure it does, and I'm excited for you. Mostly because I know how good you are. But what did you want to ask?"

"He's offering to let me stay in his house. My house. I guess it's his house now, but... There's also an apartment over the barn, but it's not very nice, and I'm not even sure that everything works. It's not furnished at all. I'd rather stay in the house, but I'm not sure that that might be too much, you know?"

"Too much in what way? Because he's a man? Doesn't he have three children?"

"Yeah. I wasn't worried about that so much, because of the kids. It's not like we would be without chaperones and living together. But I don't know... Wouldn't I be interrupting his family time?"

"Maybe he's looking for a babysitter?"

"I don't think so, his kids are old enough that they don't really need one. I think the youngest is nine. So it's not like he would need that."

"Maybe he's looking for a housekeeper."

"He does have a lovely kitchen." She paused. "My old kitchen." It was so hard to remember that it wasn't hers anymore. "That's something else I'm concerned about. If I'm living there, will I feel like it should be mine? Will I forget that it's not mine anymore? It will feel weird to not be in charge of what happens to my house. And what if the kids destroy it? And he allows it? Will I be able to just stand there and take it?"

"Those are good questions to ask yourself. I'm not sure I'll be able to answer them for you though. You're probably the only one with the answers to those questions."

"Yeah. I don't know. I guess... I guess it will be a little bit depressing to be there and know that it'll never be mine again."

"Maybe you can flip that thought."

"How so?" She drew down her brow, unsure what she meant.

"Look at it as a positive."

"How?" she asked, confused.

"Well, if the septic system backs up, it's not your baby. If the electricity goes out, you don't have to worry about it. If the roof needs to be replaced, it doesn't come out of your pocket. I mean, sure, it's nice to own it, but you have no responsibility at all. Just all the benefits of living there. And... If he's being honest and doesn't charge you, you can only benefit."

"Wow. I never thought about it like that. Instead of focusing on what I don't have, focus on what I do. Everything I want, and none of the responsibility that goes with it. I wouldn't have any bills. None. Unless one of the horses got sick."

"Yeah. And then you might make a hard decision, because sending your horse down to have an operation that only had a fifty-percent success rate maybe wasn't the best choice you've ever made."

She'd told Sunny all about what had led her to be so far in debt that she had to sell, and part of her wished she wouldn't have, because she didn't need that rubbed in, except maybe she did. Maybe she needed to be reminded that sometimes she had to make the hard decisions.

"Yeah. If I could go back and do that over..." She sighed. "I'd like to say I'd make the choice I know I need to make, but there was just something inside of me that didn't want to let Princess go, I wanted to do everything I could to save her."

"And I totally get that. But sometimes you have to make that tough choice."

"I know."

"I say go for it. If you're asking me. But if you just need to use me as a sounding board, keep talking." She stood back, with the tray pressed against her stomach, as though she were willing to wait all day to listen and be a sounding board.

"I think I'm leaning toward saying yes. He is going to be here after closing time on Wednesday, and we're going to chat about it more then."

"I'll try to make sure that I'm here early so you can knock off if he comes before that."

"You are going to be in the parade."

"The parade isn't going to last all night. I'll get back, go upstairs, change my clothes, and be back down and throw my soul into my other favorite thing."

"All right. No rush, because I told him I was working, but that sounds good to me. Maybe we can get something figured out."

"I really hope you can. I know that having you here is a blessing, but you're not doing what you were born to do. And I think that's sad. This could possibly be God opening a window or a door and hoping that you'll head through it. Who knows what's going to be on the other side."

They sounded like prophetic words.

Chapter Twelve

"I like riding in the parade better than I like watching it," Larissa said as they stood while the string trio went by, playing Christmas carols. He loved the trio and could sit and listen to it for hours, but he looked down at his daughter.

"I know." He put a hand on her head and then slid it down to her shoulder and pulled her against him.

When had she gotten so tall? She came up to his chest, and before he knew it, she was going to be a young lady, and he wasn't ready for it.

"I wish Summer was still here, because I wanted to ride in the parade too," Robert said from his other side.

He ruffled Robert's hair. "Who knows. Maybe the Lord will bring her back."

He, for one, couldn't wait to go talk to her. She hadn't texted him at all, and he had no idea what she thought. But the more he thought about it, the more he liked it. The idea of her coming back, of her being able to run her horse therapy from his stable. Sure, it would limit what the kids could do from the barn, but if the business continued to go well, maybe they could build another, smaller barn in back, where the kids could keep the riding horses. Although, if Summer was able to get the horses that they loved from their therapy sessions back, he doubted that they'd want to get different horses. But maybe he could be wrong. Maybe Summer would help him pick horses out that wouldn't be too expensive but would be perfect for his children.

Lord, this seems like the perfect solution to me, but if it is, You're going to have to convince her.

He paused in his prayer, as his children started to pick up candy from the driver of the fire truck who was throwing it out.

Maybe, maybe it wasn't just him wanting to do what God wanted him to do, but maybe he had some ulterior motives.

He didn't want to think that, but it was true. He had trouble getting Summer out of his mind. He supposed it was attraction, something he hadn't felt for a really long time. Something he didn't trust, either. After all, he'd been attracted to Desire, and look where that had gotten him—cheated on, and then she died of cancer.

He wasn't looking to get married again, wasn't looking to try to figure out how to blend his family together, and Summer was younger. She might want a family of her own, and he wasn't sure how he felt about having more children. After all, his youngest child was nine, that was an awful big gap to have, and...listen to him thinking. He'd barely even talked to the woman, she thought he was a nutcase, and here he was thinking about having children with her.

He shook his head and waved at Judd and Terry as they drove by driving the horses and pulling the wagon behind them. It was full of church kids. They had offered to allow his children to ride in the wagon too, but they had all declined. They wanted to stand with their dad, and Larissa had said that it wouldn't be the same if she wasn't on Cricket.

Maybe just for Larissa's sake, he would pray that Summer would decide to take him up on his offer.

Although, he checked out the apartment above the stable, and if she stayed, it was going to have to be in the house. The apartment was in pretty rough shape, as she had said she thought it was.

Plus, there were no furnishings at all in it, and she'd have to figure out something for a bed and a chair or table or something.

It seemed like the parade lasted an awful long time, but his kids enjoyed it and were sad when it was over. As he had arranged, his mom came to take them home after they'd walked around the festival some. He left her with some cash, thankful again that his business was doing so well, and his promise that he wouldn't be too late. He had not wanted to tell anyone what he was thinking about, because he didn't want his children to get their hopes up. He had just told his mom that he had to talk to someone about some business, and she had accepted that. He didn't tell her that it was Summer and that he was thinking about her moving in.

Regardless, once he had waved goodbye to his children, he crossed the street and moseyed down to the bakeshop. He knew she wasn't going to be able to get off for another couple of hours, but he didn't have anything else he wanted to do. And... There was something about her that drew him.

Maybe it wasn't wise for him to have someone like that in his house, when he seemed to have trouble not thinking about her.

He pushed that thought aside immediately. He didn't want to not have her. The idea was too hard to contemplate.

There was a bench not far from the shop, and he sat down, nodding at people as they passed and watching the parents of children, a couple that walked by holding hands, several that were pushing strollers, and some that had children bouncing around eating candy from the parade and probably so far up into the stratosphere on a sugar high that they would never go to bed that night.

It wasn't long after that someone carrying a cello came by, gave him an interesting glance, almost as though she were trying to place him, although he didn't recognize her other than as the woman who had played the cello in the parade, and maybe she was the owner of the shop, since she took a turn shortly after she passed him and went in the front door.

Maybe she was putting her cello away, and maybe Summer would be off sooner than he thought. Somehow the idea made him excited enough to stand up. He paced a bit, stood out of the way while a couple with two dogs on leashes walked by, and then he moseyed into the shop.

Sure enough, the woman who had walked by was behind the counter along with Summer. They were chatting and waiting on customers.

He stood in the back, a little bit beyond the crowd, and just watched. Summer's ponytail swung behind her as she smiled at the guests and competently filled their orders.

Maybe she was just one of those people who were good at whatever they did.

He kinda thought that that would be true. Or maybe it was just she put everything she had into everything that she did, as it came out well. He liked that idea better. Because he could see where she had put her heart and soul into helping his children. Even to the point of doing it without pay, just because she cared. Those kinds of people were few and far between, and he knew that having someone like that as a friend was not something that happened to a person every day.

Were they friends?

He wasn't sure she would say that they were, but hopefully after this evening, she would answer in the affirmative. And if she moved in with him and his children, surely they would be good friends. He would try to make sure of it. If he could on his end. Although, he hadn't considered that maybe she would be bitter about having to live in the house that she used to own as basically a renter who didn't pay rent.

Thinking that maybe he should have talked to someone before he made such a crazy offer, he realized that the time for getting advice was over, since she had spotted him, gave him a little wave, and then talked to the woman beside her before she pulled her apron off over her head, hung it up, and waved goodbye.

She came around the counter, and before he knew it, she was standing in front of him.

Chapter Thirteen

*S*ummer took a deep breath and tried to look friendly, not scared. She was nervous, and she couldn't explain exactly why. He was the one who had propositioned her. She was supposed to be giving a yes or no answer. It wasn't supposed to be her hoping that he was going to take her.

But still, her hands trembled as she tried to unobtrusively wipe them on her jeans. She'd taken a little extra time with her hair, brushing it until it shone and then ruining the effect by putting it all up in a ponytail for work.

She didn't know why either. It was silly. She just...wanted to look her best for this man.

"Hey," she said as she stopped in front of him, offering him half a smile.

"Hey," he said in return, seeming to be as tongue-tied as she was. Then, almost as though he shook himself, he jerked his head. "Are you off for the night? Want to walk for a bit?"

"Yes. I think the crazy crowds have dissipated some, and Sunny said that if she needed me, she'd text me."

"All right. Then let's head out. Did you get supper?" he asked, and she wasn't sure if he was offering her supper or just wanted to know if he needed to wait while she got something.

"I had a croissant earlier and a cup of tea. I'm good." She paused, wondering if maybe he was hungry. "Did you eat?"

"Yeah. I had my kids here earlier. We watched the parade. We grabbed a bite before that. Health food, that included funnel cakes and candied apples."

"Mmm. Fair food. It's so good."

"I know, right?" he said, chuckling a little.

They walked along side by side until they reached the edge of town and the last bench.

The crowds were much thinner here. It was just people walking back and forth from where they parked at the swimming pool parking lot, which was closed for the season.

"Is it good to sit here?" he asked, indicating the bench.

"Sure," she said, having used the walk to try to arrange her thoughts in order. She'd written down a list of things that she thought they ought to have in an agreement between them, but she didn't really want a lawyer. She wanted just their signatures and their agreement. Maybe that was a dangerous way to do it, but she didn't like to have a whole bunch of legal mumbo jumbo between her and the people she dealt with. She had to have the kids that she gave therapy to sign a waiver, even though the law in the state of Virginia said that anyone who was working around horses admitted that they were dangerous and they could get hurt, and they would not hold the barn owners liable. Regardless, there still needed to be an agreement, but she kept it as simple as she could.

But she didn't want to have legal stuff any more than they needed to.

"So, have you been okay the last two days?" he asked, not seeming to know where to start their conversation either. He rubbed his hands together, then clasped them and set them in his lap, before shifting a bit and stretching his legs out and pressing them.

She was sitting far enough away from him that he could put his hand up on the back bench and not touch her at all, and that seemed to be a comfortable position for him. She wanted to squirm, but she made herself sit still, slightly tilted toward him with her hands clasped in her lap, too. She would not give in to these nerves and whatever weird feeling she was having around him. Which she decided had to be mostly gratitude, for the generous offer he had given her.

"I think good. I hope you have too?"

"I have."

"Did the kids have fun watching the parade?"

"Larissa was disappointed, because she said she'd rather be in the parade riding a horse than watching the parade beside me."

"Ouch," she said, wrinkling up her nose, and he laughed.

"Yeah, I guess it was a bit of an insult, but it made me more hopeful that you would say yes to my proposition."

"Well, yes. But I did think that we probably ought to discuss how it will look. I mean, I can't just live there and not do anything. And you have rules for your house and that type of thing."

"And you need some kind of assurance that I'm not going to rip the rug out from underneath you the second I feel like it since you're trying to do your business out of my home."

"Well, yeah, I guess I was hoping for some kind of lease agreement or something."

"I wrote down a few ideas, but I didn't go to a lawyer, because... That just seems like...I don't know, not something I want to do. I guess I'd rather get taken advantage of than feel like I have to go and have a whole bunch of legal papers to sign."

"Same," she said, feeling really good about this all of a sudden. He felt the same as she did about lawyers, which was a little bit of distrust mixed with a lot of distaste. Not that lawyers couldn't be good people, just, Christians weren't supposed to need to have a lawyer between them.

"All right, sounds like we're in agreement on that. Like I said, I did take the time to write a few things down." He reached into his shirt pocket and pulled out a folded piece of paper.

She laughed and reached into her back pocket and pulled out her folded piece of paper.

They held them up, looking at each other's papers and then bursting into laughter.

"I'm not sure whether this is a good sign, that we think alike, or whether I should be scared," he said.

"Same. This is just too uncanny. I was not expecting you to show up with a list."

"I was not expecting that from you either."

They exchanged papers and then sat for a bit while they read each other's.

Her eyes skimmed over it, then she read it more slowly. Everything he had on his paper was to protect her. That they would have a signed lease agreement that she could use the barn, as long as she agreed that the barn could be used by his children when she was not giving therapy sessions.

That she would continue therapy for his children, and he would be paying for it.

She smiled at that. He had written that she would have the run of the house, except for the occupied bedrooms, and she could choose which ever unoccupied bedroom she wanted to stay in, unless she wanted to stay above the stable, but he had a note that there were a lot of things that needed to be fixed and he was hoping that she would choose to stay in the house because he didn't want to put the money he was intending to use to purchase horses into fixing up the apartment.

She could get on board with that.

She read down through the rest of them and then looked up.

He had finished reading hers and was waiting.

"You first?" he said, lifting his brow like he was giving her the option. Which he was.

"All right. All these sound good to me. I'll choose a bedroom, and then you don't have to spend money on the apartment above the stable. I knew there were some things that needed to be fixed there."

"I'm not sure how much I will get into doing it. I also saw some rodent droppings, and I heard some scratching in the walls. So I don't think you want to be there until we do a thorough extermination."

"You're correct about that," she said, smiling.

"Thought so," he said.

"All right, this lease agreement sounds good to me. Should it be six months or a year?"

"We can make it whatever you want. I have zero intention of standing in your way over that. Really, the only plans I had for the barn were for the kids to have horses there, and I was thinking that I might just build a small barn behind the house and the kids can keep their horses there, and that way you would have the entire barn in the front for yourself."

"I hate to see you do that, but that would be really nice, because I hate the idea that the kids couldn't use the stable while I'm there. Probably the only thing that I would want for them to do would be to not bother my clients and me wherever we are. For example, if we are in the ring riding, they could be in the stable. That's not a problem. I just need to be able to have uninterrupted time with my clients," she said, lifting her hands and spreading them out, hoping that he understood what she was saying.

"I totally get that. That's the reason I don't often take my kids to work with me. I can't be dealing with my children while I'm trying to deal with a client. They deserve my undivided attention, because they're putting money down in my business, and I should be making sure that they get the service they're expecting. But if my kids are there, I want to be giving them attention."

"From one business owner to another, thank you for understanding."

He nodded his head. "The kids are old enough that they understand. If they were three or four or something like that, it'd be tough to tell them and expect them to listen, but Robert, even though he's the youngest, understands that he has to wait until the adults are done speaking until he can get the attention of whoever it is that he needs to talk to."

"I agree. Your children are very well behaved, and I've never had any trouble with them at all. I really wasn't worried about that, but I appreciate you being considerate that way."

"No problem. That's the whole point. I don't want to see you lose your business and your clients and everything that you've built, and that's pretty much where my thoughts were going when I wrote out the list."

"Everything on here is for me. That's...more than I expected."

"I wanted to be fair."

"There are some things we have to do to be fair for you."

"Well, you have those all down here. You'll buy the groceries every week. And do all the cooking. Are you sure that's not too much?"

"I assumed that Larissa would help me. She said that her grandma taught her to bake and she enjoyed it. But she and I can talk about that, and maybe we can come to an agreement and just let you know, so if there's no supper on the table and it's Larissa's turn to make it, then you will not be mad at me."

"All right. I like that idea. My mom made us cook when we were little, and with my wife...getting sick, it came in handy." His voice kind of got lower, and she understood that he must be feeling a lot of pain every time he thought about his late wife. It made her sad, but it also made her curious. She really didn't know a whole lot about his wife or about how they met or anything like that, and she suddenly found herself immensely curious and wanting to know everything.

But this wasn't the time. They were talking about something completely different, and plus, that was too personal.

She definitely didn't want to go there.

He looked back down the list and said, "So you just want two months' notice if I need to sell or if you need to move, and you're offering to do some light cleaning, but I don't expect you to clean up after my children."

"I need to do something to earn my keep. I can't just live there and not pay anything."

"You gave my kids free therapy for an entire year. I can certainly house you without you having to do anything to pay for it. And you're already getting groceries and cooking."

"All right. We don't have to say that's included, as long as you don't forbid me from doing it. I occasionally like to clean, when I need to do something that allows me to think. You know?"

"I understand that. Sometimes I need to go out to the garage and tinker around in order to get my thoughts in order. Just give my hands something to do without my brain needing to be engaged."

"That's exactly right. It's a good way to describe it. Some movement, but not needing to have your brain engaged so you can think about something."

"I think I read somewhere that movement helps us to think."

"Sometimes. Sometimes I think better when I'm just sitting still. I guess... Can it depend on mood, maybe?"

"I think that's a woman's prerogative?" he said, a little hesitantly like he was afraid that he might be stepping into territory he wasn't supposed to be in.

She laughed, letting him know that it wasn't going to bother her whatever he said.

"All right, so we have that we need an agreement on the list. Can you get a lawyer to write an agreement that we both can sign?"

"I definitely think it would be a good idea for us to have a signed agreement between us, but I'm just peachy for it to be between you and me. And then...if I don't keep my word, you can come after me however you want to, but I'm not going to hire a lawyer and get really upset if you don't do what you say you're going to do. I... I guess I just believe that there shouldn't be lawyers between Christians."

"That's a dangerous position and not a popular one, but the Bible does say that Christians should not sue other Christians at law, especially in a secular court, if I understand the Bible correctly."

"That's what I understand it to say too. That we're supposed to just judge each other and not go outside to secular people in order to settle our disagreements."

He appeared thoughtful, as he nodded, running a hand over his chin, before he crossed his arms over his chest and held the paper up. "All right then, I can write something up that includes everything that we have here, and... I can have it ready by tomorrow if you need me to."

"I guess that would be another question, how soon do you want to move on this?"

"Did you find out if you can get your horses back?"

"I thought I might be getting the cart ahead of the horse a little bit, so to speak." She chuckled a little, and he laughed along with her. "But I did call about them. I can get them all back. I didn't spend the money. I didn't need it, since you paid more for the farm than what I was asking. So, I can buy them back...as soon as I can arrange transportation." She had a trailer and could transport them, but the buyers had picked them up, so she just had to figure out if they could bring them back, or when she'd need to fit it in her schedule.

"All right then. I'm ready to move today, but I don't want you to make your employer mad."

"She's not going to be mad at me, but you're right. I don't want to leave her high and dry, although she didn't have an employee before I came, and I've only been working three days. Still, she was kind enough to give me a job when I needed one, and I want to treat her right."

"That's fair. You want to see how long of a notice she needs?"

"I'll do that. It won't be longer than two weeks, but I wouldn't be surprised if she says she doesn't need a notice at all."

They sat there a little bit, both of them seeming to think about everything, and then she decided that maybe she should ask a couple of the questions she was curious about.

"I... I don't want to overstep, because we just agreed to me living in your house, but that doesn't give me the right to any of your personal history."

"It's open for discussion, if you're interested."

"I guess I was just thinking that I might like to know a little bit about you. Considering that we're going to be living in close quarters. I know a good bit about your children, but you are more of a mystery."

"My life's an open book, for the most part." He seemed to be thinking about something, but he didn't say anything more.

"What kind of business do you have?" she asked, figuring she would start with something simple. She wasn't sure if she wanted to try to delve into any of the things that she was super curious about, because there were things that maybe were a little bit too personal, but she did want to know a little bit more about him. After all, she really was going to be living in his house.

"I own an equipment rental company. My business is located in Harrisonburg, and that's where I lived for a while, but I really wanted the kids to be able to grow up in Mistletoe Meadows. It's much smaller, and you know how it is. A close-knit community with people who watch out for each other. We like each other, and we take care of each other. Harrisonburg isn't that big, but it's a completely different feel. Although, I don't think my business would be a success in Mistletoe Meadows."

"Are you going to be traveling back and forth?"

"No. I... Maybe you heard that it was on the brink of bankruptcy right after my wife died?"

"I did hear that."

"My office manager was embezzling money. Suffice it to say she was accepting cash from clients and then keeping those rentals off the books. She was also not paying bills when they were due, and part of the reason was there wasn't a whole lot of money coming in, since she was getting everything paid in cash."

"How did you figure that out? There would be no paper trail."

"She made an offer to someone who considered themselves my friend, thankfully. It was kind of surprising to me how many people didn't consider themselves my friend enough to feel like they needed to tell me what was going on. Or at least alert me to the fact that it was strange she was wanting cash payments. But this guy did, and I was able to report it to the police who did some undercover work, caught her red-handed, and while she didn't get charged for everything she did, we can look at the books and see that she probably took over half of the money that my business made for the last six months of my wife's life."

"I think it takes a special kind of person to embezzle money from a man who has three children and is losing their mother and his wife to cancer. Wow."

"Yeah. I guess I thought the same thing. Who could do that to someone, right?" He gave a wan smile. "Well, I found someone who could, and I hired her and put her in a position of authority. I believe I've been a little bit more careful this time, and I've made sure that my employees know that there are cameras, with sound, so I can check on my business anytime."

Chapter Fourteen

"But you're not going to be there daily?" Summer lifted her shoulder, watching a couple stroll by toward the parking lot, leaving the festival hand in hand and whispering to each other. They looked so happy and in love, she almost forgot what she was going to say. "I'm not trying to figure out when you're going to be there and when you're not, exactly. I have no nefarious intentions. I was just curious."

"I can let you know what my schedule looks like, although right now, it's wide open." Gilbert laughed a little. "I don't think it's going to stay that way for long."

"I hope not. I did call about the horses, and I know I can get them back, but I figured I might be being a little bit too optimistic if I called my clients and told them that I was back in business. But I can guarantee you that I'll be doing that first thing in the morning. Once I talk to Sunny and find out how long she wants me to work and what kind of notice she wants me to give."

"That makes me happy. I'm glad you think that you're going to be able to get back into business that easily."

"I'm hoping."

"To answer your question, I shouldn't need to be in the office at all, but I do want to keep my finger on things. It's too easy for people to run away with things, if I'm not there and they know I'm not going to be there keeping an eye on them. At the same time, the whole point of me rebuilding the business, and getting it so that it was making money again, was so that I could spend time with my children. As you probably know, since my mom and my sisters were the ones who had been handling the kids, I haven't been around a whole lot for the last year, as I did that. But I promised myself that whole year that once I got things under control, I was going to step back and spend as much time as I could with my kids. I can't believe Lucas is twelve. Before I know it, he's going to be out of the house, and it's going to make me sad that I missed so much of his life."

"I do think you have to cherish the time you get to spend with your kids, because it's fleeting."

"Yes. I'm starting to figure that out. How did you get to be so wise? You don't have any children of your own."

"No. I love kids, and I always thought I'd have some, but it just hasn't been the way the Lord's worked my life out so far." She didn't say anything more. She really did want children. And it felt like that opportunity was slipping away. "Maybe I focused a little bit too much on my career and allowed the opportunities that I had to possibly develop a relationship that could lead to marriage and children slip by."

"Or maybe God was just having you do something else until the right one comes along."

"Like you did with your wife?" she asked, hoping he answered, because she was extremely curious.

"I suppose. Although, maybe not. We were high school sweethearts and got married shortly after I graduated from high school. I think I was twenty. And she was nineteen."

"Wow. So young."

"Yeah. I don't have anything against kids getting married young. In fact, I think maybe the whole idea of people needing to wait to mature is not as good of an idea as what everybody thinks it is. You don't need to see the world first, or fulfill yourself, or whatever. If you're following the Lord, He'll provide whatever it is you need, and you will be fulfilled in Him. I think we've totally missed that, especially as Christians, and we have a tendency to speak the way the world speaks, instead of the way we really should speak, according to the Bible."

"I guess I hadn't thought about it that way, but when you say it like that, I have to agree. If we are following God, and we commit to our spouse, it shouldn't matter how old we are when we marry, if we've been brought up to keep our commitments and do what we say we're going to do."

"Exactly."

She laughed to herself that they had gotten so far off-topic. How were they talking about relationships and discussing what God wanted? She found she agreed with him, which surprised her even more.

"Maybe you're not as old as I thought. You must be thirty?"

"Thirty-two."

"I see."

"So, you know how old I am. Can I ask how old you are? Even though I know I'm not supposed to ask that or your weight."

"I don't think I'm going to tell you my weight, but I'm twenty-seven."

"I don't think the world has passed you by at that age. You're young yet."

"Just five years younger than you."

"That explains why I didn't know you. My mom said the kids were taking lessons and you had gone to my school, but I was probably out of high school before you started in that building."

"Since both of us grew up in Mistletoe Meadows, we would have gone to the same school, but you're right. I was a while after you, although I knew about the McBrides, and I probably knew you, although over the years, I'd forgotten."

"So you knew Isadora?"

"Yeah. And Roland. I think one was in the grade above me and one was in the grade below."

"But you managed to avoid being stuck in a grade with a McBride. Life is good."

"I guess. I didn't realize that I was lucky that way."

"Did you always know that you wanted to work with horses?"

"I did. At least I hoped that I got to. Since I was an only child, I did a lot of work on the farm. Back when I was growing up, there was more acreage, which Dad sold off when Mom started remodeling the house. But then he had to remortgage the house, because it cost more than what they thought it was going to. The nice part about that is Mom didn't cut any corners and everything is top-of-the-line, and it's done very well. It's just...very expensive."

"I got that impression. I was really impressed when I was walking through. The designer, whoever it was, did a great job of not completely obliterating the fact that there was an addition put on, but everything flows so well it doesn't feel jarring, the way some additions do."

"I agree completely. I was in some of my friends' houses, where you have basically three houses slapped together. It's weird, although those houses definitely have character."

"That's true, they do. A lot more character than modern-day houses, although if someone wanted to give me a brand-new house, I would not turn them down."

"Same. But I do love the character that an older house has."

"I do too. The wide staircases, the natural light, and the beautiful wood are just some of the things that really impressed me when I walked through the first time."

"I kind of wished Dad wouldn't have sold all the grounds, because it was a nice working farm, but the twenty acres that goes with it is enough to keep a few horses and give you some room to ride around."

"That's kind of what I thought. Did you help him make hay?"

She couldn't believe how comfortable she found him as they chatted about their childhoods and different things that came up. He talked a little more about his wife's cancer, and how difficult it was for the children, and how they thought they had it beat until they started getting more bad news every time they went to the doctor. She ended up telling him about the two serious boyfriends she had in college, although neither one of them were interested in moving to a small town like Mistletoe Meadows, and she ended up ending her relationships with both of them. She told him about how she had been able to finish her degree online, other than her clinicals, and even those had been things that she had been able to do not very far from home.

They found out that they were both homebodies.

Of course, his upbringing was a lot different since he had five siblings, and he talked about that a little bit.

By the time she looked around, she realized it was almost midnight and the festival was practically deserted.

"My goodness, can you believe the time?" she said, standing up abruptly, when she saw it was almost midnight.

"Wow. I had no idea. I told my mom I wouldn't be late. She's watching the kids."

"Your mom is amazing. One of my favorite people, and someday I hope I can grow up to be just like her."

"Yeah. She can be a little bit intimidating because she's so… wonderful. You know?"

"I guess I don't find her intimidating, because she's always been very friendly and sweet, quick to laugh at herself, and I've never seen her get upset or impatient."

"It's been a long time since I've seen that, too. But she does have a voice, and when she uses that tone, you know she means business, and people jump to do whatever it is she wants. She doesn't use it very often, but it's very effective."

"I would imagine it would be, if she was a single mom raising six kids."

"Yeah. She was quite a woman."

"Well, hopefully she doesn't have to use her tone on you whenever you come walking in at midnight, and after telling her that she wouldn't be there for very long."

"The kids are old enough that they really don't need a babysitter, but I like to have an adult around just to keep an eye on them. I... Maybe I'm a little overprotective that way."

"Somebody had to take them home anyway. And something tells me your mom doesn't mind keeping an eye on them."

They had started walking back toward the bakery.

"I assume you live over the bakery right now?"

"I do."

"All right, I'll walk you home, since I kept you out so late."

Him saying that made it almost seem like a date, when it wasn't anything close. But... She had never been out on a date when she lost track of time so thoroughly as they chatted about everything and anything.

True to his word, he walked her to the bakery, which had a closed sign hanging on the window.

"This might be a stupid question, but you have a key, right?"

"I do. And if I don't, I have my phone, and Summer will let me in."

"All right. If you don't mind, I'll wait until I see you walk in. Mistletoe Meadows is as safe as any town, but there is always a lunatic around somewhere."

"Unfortunately, that's true," she said as she pulled the key out of her pocket and put it in the lock of the door that was directly beside the window in the bakery.

"I had a really great time, thank you so much for your offer and for being willing to talk to me, and... Yeah. Thank you." She wanted to say she was looking forward to moving in with him, but that sounded a little weird, and for some reason, she couldn't think of any other words.

"Thank you. And I'm sorry I didn't think of this earlier. I should have. It wasn't very nice of me to only be thinking about myself."

"Nobody thought that you should be offering your home or not buying a place just because I needed it. Honest."

"I thought about that, but then... Christians are supposed to be different, right? I shouldn't have been just thinking about myself, even though I'm the protector and provider of my family and my children should come first. I should have been thinking about a way I could help you, that would enable you to do what you wanted."

"I don't know about that. I guess I disagree on the one hand, but on the other hand, I do agree that Christians are supposed to be different, and too many times we're not. We're just as selfish as everyone around us, and people have to look really hard with a microscope almost in order to actually see Jesus in us. It shouldn't be that way."

"You're absolutely right about that. I don't want them to have to use a microscope. I want Jesus to radiate off me in such a way that people barely have to glance at me before they know that Jesus is here." He tapped his heart.

She nodded, charmed, despite herself. The evening had been... magical might have been a little too strong of a word, but it had been wonderful at the very least, and to know that he felt that way about the Lord made it even better.

She was completely and totally content and happy about moving in with him and his three children. And even more relaxed and unafraid about opening her business back up, even though she no longer owned the stable. She was confident that he would treat her right, no matter what happened.

"I'll see you soon," she said as the lock clicked and she opened the door.

"Thank you. You'll let me know if anything comes up, right?"

She nodded. "You can expect a text from me tomorrow. I'll tell you what Sunny said, and I'll wait until after I know when the horses are coming to give you the lowdown on them."

"Sounds good. Good night," he said, but he made no move to leave.

"Good night," she said, and then she had the strangest urge to move closer to him, like...like there would be a good night kiss.

But it wasn't a date, not anything close, and she resisted that urge and turned, maybe a little faster than what she was planning on, and hurried in the door, closing it behind her.

Wow. She had not been expecting that.

Chapter Fifteen

Gilbert was still a little bemused the next day after he had sent the kids off to school.

He had checked in with his business, went over the recordings of the night before, checked the numbers, and decided that he would take a walk around the property.

He had just gone outside when Judd, his brother-in-law, pulled up to the porch.

Gilbert stood on the top step, watching him park, wondering what in the world he might want.

"Good morning," Judd said as he got out of the truck.

"Good morning. Nice day," Gilbert said, looking at the brilliant blue sky and feeling the gentle breeze, which did not feel chilly in the slightest, despite the fact that it was almost Thanksgiving.

"I thought I'd come out and see the place. I was going to wait for Terry, but she told me to go ahead and scope it out for her, and let her know what she needed to see."

"You're welcome anytime. You don't need me to give you the tour. Although if you want me to, I can."

"She thinks you should have an open house or something."

"Maybe I'll host Thanksgiving here."

"That's an excellent idea. I know Terry would get on board with that, and as long as your mom's okay with it, I can't think of any better way for the family to see the place."

"All right then, I'll..." He almost said he'd check with Summer, but he didn't figure Judd probably knew he was going to be hosting her. For lack of a better word. He hated to say that she would be living with him, because that made it sound like...there was more there than what there was, although after last night, he almost wondered if maybe it wasn't so far-fetched for him to hope that there might eventually be more.

She was one of the most interesting people he talked to in a long time, and he didn't think he'd ever get tired of listening to her. She seemed interested in him, and they agreed on so many things, plus they made each other laugh.

It was far less than what he would have needed to date a girl back in the day, but... He wasn't sure that he and Summer would have that kind of relationship, even though it felt that way to him. Maybe she saw him as an older man, even though there were only five years between them, but he had three kids, and that kind of put him in a completely different category than what she was.

"I think I can wait for my tour until Thanksgiving, if that's what you're going to do."

"I think so. You want to hang here, sit down on the porch swing, and chat a bit?"

"Don't mind if I do. It's been a busy few weeks, and I kind of feel like a break is a good idea."

"I don't have tea or anything, but you can have a glass of water if you want."

"I didn't come expecting you to wait on me hand and foot. I just thought I'd visit you in your new digs. See if there is anything you're doing that you need a hand with."

Judd was just that kind of guy. Always willing to lend a hand, which was saying something, since the guy was handy and could fix pretty much anything.

They sat down on the swing together and were quiet for just a bit.

"What are your plans for the place?" Judd eventually said.

"There's only twenty acres with it, so it's not like I'm going to be able to farm it or anything. And…" Was it okay to tell Judd what he was going to do? Judd would tell Terry, but it wouldn't go any further if he didn't want it to. But if the family was coming for Thanksgiving, they were going to see Summer there, and regardless, his kids were never going to keep it a secret.

Not that he thought it should be a secret.

"You know the woman who owned it before, Summer?"

"Sure, I've seen Summer a bunch, when Terry and I took your kids to their therapy sessions. Great girl. She was excellent with the children. If your kids have processed the death of their mother, I think you can really thank her."

"I agree with you. They are attached to her, attached to the horses, and believe it or not, they cried when they learned that she was going to have to sell them."

"I believe it. It's funny, because Lucas has developed kind of into that strong, silent type, but he loved Thatcher."

Gilbert was impressed Judd knew the name of Lucas's horse. It probably said a lot about what Lucas had talked to Judd about and what Judd had observed when he was watching the kids at their sessions.

"He did. And that, along with a few other reasons, prompted me to see if Summer wanted to come back and stay here, and continue with her therapy business. She did so much for my kids and didn't charge me anything. I felt like it was the least I could do."

"Wow. Did she take you up on it?"

"She did. I talked to her about it last night, and I should be getting a text from her sometime today letting me know when she's going to be moving in."

"Is she going to be able to get her horses back?"

"She was very confident that she would be able to do that."

"Is she going to be living here?" Judd moved a hand, indicating the house.

"There are six bedrooms upstairs, so plenty for her to choose from, so yeah. She's going to pick a bedroom, and she will be here, buying groceries, cooking, and I'm not charging her rent."

He added that last part because he knew that Judd might be latching onto the fact that they were unmarried and living in the same house. It didn't look the greatest, Gilbert knew, but the kids would be there as chaperones, and they weren't staying in the same bedroom. She was a renter. She was leasing the barn. It wasn't a sin.

"That's nice of you. Probably because she didn't charge you for the therapy sessions."

"Yeah. That was a great example to me. I...know, as a business owner, that you can't just give away everything for free, but when you see a need, you can work to fulfill it and trust God to take care of you. So maybe he used her to take care of me, and now I'm taking care of her."

"I see. It was probably really hard for her to give up this place, considering that it's been in her family for so long."

"Yeah." He realized that wasn't really something that they had talked about.

"You don't think she's taking advantage of you?" Judd said slowly after a while.

"What? Because I own her house now?"

"Sure. It's probably hard for her to leave it, and then, hey, she found a way to stay on the family property."

"But I still own it. She doesn't have any say in it." He wasn't sure where Judd was going with that.

"I see. I guess that sounds fine, if you're not sharing the property."

"No. Nothing like that."

"So... She doesn't have designs on you?" Judd finally said.

Now Gilbert understood where Judd was going.

"You think that she's trying to be romantically interested in me to get me to...marry her? So she'd get her house back?"

"Is that so far-fetched?"

"You know her. Would you say that she's that kind of person?"

"No. I wouldn't say she's that kind of person at all, but I can see other people saying that."

"I see." He was so tempted to say that he did feel romantically inclined toward her, but he didn't want to share that. Not really, not when she was going to be moving into the house, and it already looked not the greatest. But, he was interested in Judd's opinion.

"What do you think of her?" he finally asked.

"I think she's one of the best girls I know. Terry and I both said about how good she is with your kids, how great she is with her job, how much she cares about people, and she doesn't hesitate to go the extra mile, or two or three. Just like she gave your kids therapy for free, she often went over the allotted time, and not just with your kids but with the kids who were there before them. She's just... She's an impressive woman."

"Then why are you insinuating that she might be after me romantically to get the farm?"

"I just know that some people will say that about her, and I guess that was my way of warning you."

"I am more concerned about what they are going to say when they find out she's living here."

"There's that too."

They didn't say anything more, because Gilbert wasn't sure what to do about it. He'd already offered for her to stay, and he wasn't going to go back on that offer. But he knew that there would be some people in town who would frown on it, even if they said that they were sleeping in different bedrooms, and there was absolutely nothing going on.

The Bible did say that a Christian was supposed to abstain from all appearance of evil.

He'd have to think about that and see if he could come up with something, because he didn't want there to be any appearance of evil, but he also wasn't going to not offer her exactly what he had or take his offer back.

Just then, his phone buzzed with a text.

> Sunny asked me to work the weekend, then I'm done. I can buy all of my horses back, and Thatcher arrives next week. I could move in on Monday, if that works for you?

Gilbert stared at his phone, thinking about what Judd had just said to him and knowing that there was some type of attraction on his side anyway, toward Summer. But he would just have to be careful, and... If it developed into something more, he was going to have to be honest and upright. However that looked.

He looked up to see Judd with his brows raised, waiting. "She's coming on Monday."

Chapter Sixteen

"*I* was so excited about having a roommate and friend to do stuff with, and you no sooner get here than you're leaving. I hope it's okay for me to be disappointed," Sunny said as they walked arm in arm toward church.

"Of course. I'm disappointed too, in a way. But in another way, I'm so excited about how God worked this out. He took all of the bills and worry off my shoulders and allowed me to continue to live on my farm, rent free, the place I've always loved. I...guess it shouldn't surprise me the way the Lord worked things out, but it does."

She was so focused on how good God was that she didn't notice Mrs. Tucker until Mrs. Tucker stopped on the sidewalk right in front of them, her hands on her hips, the ever-present clipboard gripped in one of them.

"Good morning, ladies," Mrs. Tucker said, and beside her, Summer could almost feel Sunny groan.

"Sunny, I wanted to see if you would be willing to donate six dozen muffins for our Thanksgiving breakfast?"

"Wow. That's this Thursday."

"I know it's last-minute notice, but we thought we'd be able to get them from Nora's bakeshop down in Whisker Hollow, but the Baplodist church there imitated our idea, and they're having a Thanksgiving breakfast, and Nora is already booked up."

Summer bit back a smile. Sunny and Nora were good friends, but there was a friendly competition between the two of them. All Mrs. Tucker had to do was mention Nora's bakeshop, and Sunny was all in.

"Of course I'll donate them. Does it matter what kind?"

"We'd like two dozen pumpkin, three dozen blueberry, and one dozen bran." Mrs. Tucker was obviously prepared for that question.

"I need to write that down," Sunny said, grabbing her phone out and repeating the breakdown, making sure she had it right.

As Summer started to walk away, Mrs. Tucker said, "Just hold on there a second. I have a question for you too, Summer."

Summer stopped, thinking that she had almost gotten away. She just needed to be a little faster the next time.

Mrs. Tucker waited until Sunny had the order down before she turned to Summer. "I hoped that you would be able to donate your horses to the tree farm on Mondays starting after Thanksgiving. The church is sponsoring a little Christmas booth that Noah Tripp, the owner of the tree farm, has approved, and we were hoping that you would be there with your horses giving carriage rides to try to draw in a crowd. He has a carriage, but he sold his horses many years ago, as I'm sure you're aware."

Cricket and Bunny were both great buggy horses as well as riding horses, and she would have them back in time. What she found more interesting than anything was that obviously Mrs. Tucker was losing a step, since she hadn't heard that Summer had sold them.

"I can do that on Mondays. They're slow days for me with my therapy, and the one appointment that I typically have can be moved." If they came back. She had gotten her horses and arranged things with Sunny, but she hadn't been able to get a hold of all of her clients.

So far, she only had about a quarter of them back on her

schedule. She was not going to allow that to worry her. She kept reminding herself that she no longer had a farm to pay for. She could afford to work less, if she needed to. All she needed to do was make enough money to feed her horses and hopefully have a little extra so that she could give Gilbert money for rent, even though he didn't want her to. She just couldn't live there for free.

Of course, she had to buy groceries too, which she knew would be a lot more than she was used to spending, since she didn't typically cook for growing kids and a man.

"All right. I'll depend on you from now until Christmas to drive the buggy on Mondays." Mrs. Tucker blinked several times, and looked around, then she lowered her voice. "There's a nasty rumor going around that you had sold your horses, but I knew it wasn't true."

Summer wasn't quite sure what to say about that. It was true, but it wasn't true anymore, and she wasn't sure she wanted to stand there and explain it all to Mrs. Tucker, who was surely going to announce it to the entire town. She supposed the longer it took for everyone to figure out that she was living on the farm she used to own, and staying in the house with Gilbert and his three kids, the better.

Mrs. Tucker soon found someone else she needed to talk to and hurried off, leaving Summer and Sunny standing, bemused, on the sidewalk.

"Well, I didn't see that coming. I should have been watching a little better."

"Mrs. Tucker has a tendency to do that to people. I don't know how someone of her size sneaks around as easily as what she does."

"You said that so much better than I could have," Sunny said with a giggle.

They hooked arms again and continued on their way to church, smiling and chatting, and since now Sunny had six dozen muffins to make in addition to everything else, Summer told her that she would help her if she could.

As she was trying to figure out her schedule for the week and when she could come in to help bake, she heard the bells then saw the sleigh/wagon pull up in front of the church.

It was easy to pick out Gilbert's three kids as they bounded off the sleigh, but it was a little while until she noticed Gilbert standing halfway up the walk. And when she finally saw him, she realized that instead of watching his children run to him, his eyes had caught on her.

He smiled as their gazes met, and she returned it, nodding a hello.

Funny that her heart started beating an irregular rhythm and she suddenly felt like she was out of breath.

"So...that will work?" Sunny asked, and she ripped her gaze away from Gilbert. Why did he have that effect on her?

"Yes. Tuesday morning should work just fine. I only have a quarter of my clients back, and I'll just make sure I tell them this Tuesday doesn't work for me."

"I don't want you to lose work because you're helping me."

"You were willing to take me in, on such a short notice, and then have me work for a few days and I quit immediately, and you're not angry about it. Of course I'm going to help you. You couldn't have been nicer to me in any way."

Sunny just grinned. "That's what friends are for."

That made Summer's mouth turn up, and she almost forgot about Gilbert. Except, they happened to meet at the steps, getting there at the same time.

Sunny squeezed her arm, nodded a hello to Gilbert, and then hurried into the church on the heels of Gilbert's children. Leaving Gilbert and Summer standing at the steps, which were suddenly deserted.

"Good morning," he said, his voice sending shivers down her spine.

She tried not to allow that to show as she nodded serenely. "It's a beautiful morning."

"It sure is. It's been so warm this whole fall, we're going to get spoiled with all this nice weather."

"We sure are," she said, thinking about how good God had been to her. He had definitely been spoiling her.

"I wanted to offer to help tomorrow, if you have anything you need to move." He lifted his shoulder and looked a little sheepish. "It looks like you left most of the things that were in the house, but surely you took some things, and I just wanted you to know that I would be available."

"Thank you. I appreciate the offer, but everything is still in my car pretty much, other than the clothes I needed to wear. Sunny didn't have room for it, and I didn't know what to do with it."

"I really miss the plants that were in the kitchen."

Really? She had almost left them, but then she didn't want to leave more responsibility, because while plants were fairly easy to take care of, they did require watering and occasional pruning.

"I'll definitely bring them back," she said easily.

How much information did she need to give him? Should she tell him that she was going to be at the tree farm every Monday after Thanksgiving between Thanksgiving and Christmas?

Maybe that was something they could talk about eventually, but an awkward silence descended and she found herself talking just to fill it.

"My horses are coming back, although I guess I told you that in the text." They had had such an easy rapport when they spoke at the festival. Why was it so weird today?

Maybe it was because she realized after talking to him that they had so much in common, and she actually admired him. He was handsome and kind and articulate, and she saw him as a man, rather than...someone who had lost his wife.

"The stables are empty and waiting on them. I was going to fix some fence, so the pastures will be ready for them as well."

She couldn't help the widening of her eyes. He didn't need to do that. He wasn't using the pastures at all, and the only reason that he'd be fixing the fence would either be for the aesthetic effects or because he wanted to help her. After talking to him, she guessed the latter, because that was just the way he was.

"Wow. Maybe I can come and give you a hand with that fence. Once I unpack my car, I don't have anything else planned for the rest of the day. Although Tuesday I just told Sunny I would give her a hand with some muffins she has to make."

"All right. That sounds good to me. We'll plan on fixing fence on Monday around ten o'clock or so?"

"Yeah. That sounds good."

"Perfect. That gives me a chance to check in with my business and make sure everything's going okay there."

She nodded, and he said, "I guess we should go ahead in."

"Yeah," she said and somehow found herself walking up the steps, very aware of his presence beside her. She hadn't realized how much bigger he was than she, and while he didn't make her feel scared or threatened in any way, she felt petite and feminine. Which was...a little odd. And it was even more odd that she liked it. Usually she enjoyed feeling competent and in control. As she didn't particularly like the feeling of being small and dainty.

Funny how having the right person beside her made the feeling one that she cherished rather than disliked.

"Gilbert McBride!"

Mrs. Tucker came hurrying toward them from the side of the church.

Summer wasn't sure whether she should stay or whether she should run away. She figured she was saved from Mrs. Tucker, since Mrs. Tucker had already asked her for her favor of the day. But maybe she should give Gilbert and Mrs. Tucker privacy.

She was a little trapped between the two of them though, since her back was against the wall and Gilbert moved over to allow Mrs. Tucker to stand a little to her left in front of her. For her to leave would have made more of a big deal than for her to just stand there.

"Good morning, Mrs. Tucker," Gilbert said pleasantly.

"I'm so glad I caught you. I have the most wonderful news," Mrs. Tucker said, lifting both hands and pumping her fist like Gilbert was going to be excited.

Summer figured that that meant she had something extra difficult for Gilbert to do. And she tried not to giggle. After all, it wasn't kind to glory in someone else's misery. And Gilbert truly did look miserable, despite his pleasant tone.

"And what would that be?" he asked, tilting his head and seeming to feign interest.

"We have a new resident in our small town. We are so blessed to have Darla Zoubak who is moving here all the way from Washington, DC. Now, I said to myself, Helen, who would be the perfect person to show Darla around our town, and do you know whose name came to my mind immediately?"

"Roland's," Gilbert said immediately, and Summer had to stifle a laugh. Of course he would name his brother, hoping that Mrs. Tucker would go sink her claws into him.

"That was close. Right family, but it was you." She used both pointer fingers to point right at Gilbert's chest. It was a little surprising that he didn't try to duck.

"I know that you will be the perfect person to lead her around, and I don't like to be the one that reminds you of things that happened in the past, but it's been almost a year since you lost your wife, and you really need to get back in the dating scene. Darla is perfect for you. She's a professional, she works for a congressman in Washington, and she's looking for a weekend getaway. Which, of course, our town is perfect for her. She has all of next week, and so she's spending it here with us, and she somehow got my name." Mrs. Tucker put a hand on her chest and pretended to be shocked, like everyone in town wouldn't say her name as the person who knew the most about everyone, except possibly the Secret Saint.

"And she gave me a call and asked me if I could set her up with someone who not only could be a possible love interest for her weekend getaways here but also who would show her around the town and give her a good time. Automatically I thought of you. You are the best person to represent our town, and I hope you don't mind, but I gave her your name and your number, and she'll be contacting you about where you two can meet on Tuesday for you to show her everything you know about our quaint little town."

Mrs. Tucker looked so pleased with herself that Summer wasn't sure she would have been able to come up with any kind of rational argument, and... Maybe Gilbert didn't want to.

After all, Mrs. Tucker was right. It had been a year since his wife passed away, and he probably was ready to get into the dating scene again, and Darla really did sound perfect for him. After all, he had a business in a bigger town, and he was used to rubbing elbows with businesspeople, and for some reason, that made Summer, and her little horseback riding therapy thing, seem like kindergarten compared to Darla and her big-city ways. A congressman. That was impressive.

She wished she would have left whenever she had the opportunity, but to leave now would feel like slinking away, and she didn't want Gilbert to think that she was all doom and gloom just because they had spent one evening having a nice conversation together, and now he was being tapped to lead another woman around town.

"I know you're not going to let me down. Your mom will be so pleased with you being the next Mrs. Tucker of Mistletoe Meadows." Mrs. Tucker waved her hand in the air and hurried off.

"I'm not sure I was given the opportunity to decline that," Gilbert said slowly after she left.

"That's kind of the way Mrs. Tucker is. I got roped into using my horses to give carriage rides at the Christmas tree farm on Mondays between Thanksgiving and Christmas, and it didn't even occur to me to tell her no."

"That's the way she is, isn't it? You feel like you're not a good, patriotic citizen if you don't say yes to everything she asks."

"Exactly. Although… While she's talking to you, you usually don't even have time to think about declining."

"No. But when you see her coming, your instinct is to run, and I don't know why I didn't follow that instinct." He looked at her balefully. "Probably because I didn't want to leave her with you."

"I considered running, but she already got me for today, and I figured she wasn't after me, so I guess I figured I could stick around and watch her massacre someone else."

"Thanks. You could have pushed me down the steps. That would have been nicer."

"I'll remember that for next time," she said.

"All right. I guess I'm spending time with Darla what's her name on Tuesday." He didn't look very happy about it, and that did speak to her heart. Except, if he were truly interested in her, which she realized that, deep down, she was hoping he was, he would have said no unequivocally to Mrs. Tucker. "I need to go find my kids and sit down. If I don't see you after church, I'll see you tomorrow," he said as they walked into the sanctuary and prepared to go in different directions.

"Yeah. I'm looking forward to it." And she realized, no matter what he had agreed to do with Mrs. Tucker and that Darla, it was true. She really was looking forward to it.

Chapter Seventeen

onday morning, Gilbert found himself a little distracted as he got the kids off to school. Normally he enjoyed the time in the morning where he chatted with the kids, put their lunches together, and made sure that they had everything that they needed. He really did miss the time that he got to spend with his kids, and he was glad that they were back in the same house together. Although, his mom made cooking breakfast at six o'clock in the morning look easy and fun, and it was anything but.

He burned a batch of pancakes and dropped a measuring cup on the floor, breaking it.

But the kitchen was gorgeous, and Summer was coming, and he was with his children, together, and even the little annoyances couldn't dampen his anticipation of the coming day. He and Summer were going to be fixing fence together, they were going to talk some more, and... He wasn't quite sure why he was so eagerly looking forward to that. But he was.

He stood at the door while his children trooped out to wait for the bus, then hung out by the window, watching until they got on.

They were old enough that they didn't necessarily want him down there standing with them when the bus arrived. But they weren't old enough for him to totally forget about them as soon as they walked out the door.

Would they ever be that old? He really didn't think so. He couldn't imagine not caring about his kids or not wanting to see them. Maybe that was made sharper by all the time he missed with them while Desire was sick and then while he was rebuilding his business.

At the thought of his business, he walked into the library, which he'd been using as his office, and opened his laptop.

He was not looking forward to this Darla person coming, and Mrs. Tucker couldn't have picked a worse time. For the last almost year since his wife had passed away, and for almost four years before that, since he found the note where he realized she had been cheating on him, he hadn't been the slightest bit interested in women or romance. He'd put his best effort into continuing to have a good marriage, but inside he had been bitter and angry.

Being with Summer last week at the festival was the first time that he'd sat and talked to a woman and truly felt happy and understood. Like... Like there could be something more than just conversation.

And now, Mrs. Tucker had to go and put a wedge between them.

He blamed Mrs. Tucker, but it wasn't her fault at all. It was his. He could have said no. He could have looked at Summer who was standing right there and said that he had someone else in mind, and he wanted to be able to give all his attention to them.

But he didn't know how Summer felt, and he didn't want to make her uncomfortable, if all she saw was an older man who was doing something nice for her and giving her a place to stay, helping her out. Maybe even she considered him a friend.

He cringed. He didn't want to be friend zoned.

But he probably deserved it. Since he could have been a lot nicer to her, could have tried to look for ways to help her save her farm. It occurred to him that whoever was the Secret Saint around town was doing that very thing. Trying to help people, rather than bettering himself.

Not that there was anything at all wrong with bettering himself, but he couldn't really pat himself on the back for doing a kindness to Summer when he could have done a lot better, if he had been willing to put himself last.

He'd have to think about that a little more, because would that have meant he wouldn't have bought the farm after all?

And then, he felt a little God nudge. Maybe God was working this all out, and he didn't need to beat himself up about it anymore. Maybe everything was going according to the Lord's plan. That it was perfectly okay for him to buy a farm, and it was even better for him to lend a helping hand to someone, no matter how he did it.

He smiled, thinking about his Bible reading that morning and how much he appreciated just the short time he'd been back home, getting back into the Word. For far too long, he'd been neglecting it and setting it aside, and he could already see benefits of the short weeks that he'd been spending with the Lord.

A calmness, a trust in God's plan that hadn't been there before, a knowledge that it was less about him and more about knowing that God would work everything out.

He had no sooner thought that than he saw Summer's truck coming up the driveway.

He didn't know where she had her horse trailer, because he hadn't seen it along the street when he'd been walking with her, but it was hooked to her truck now as she came into view and pulled in at the barn. She backed the trailer in and unhooked it. And then she got back in her truck and drove to the house.

He should have been on his laptop, looking at his business, instead of watching Summer like some lovesick schoolboy dreaming out the school window.

She came to the back door, and he was there to meet her, opening it as she had her hand raised to knock.

"I've been watching for you," he said, thinking that was a major understatement. He'd been standing at the window watching her every move.

"I'm sorry I'm a little late. It was busy at the shop this morning, and I threw on an apron and stood behind the counter for a bit to give Sunny a break."

"She needs to hire someone."

"She's trying. She really is. She has someone starting tomorrow, but it's just so tough. People either don't want to work, or they can't do something as simple as showing up to work on time, let alone actually being able to physically do the job."

"I would think it wouldn't be that hard to sell muffins and scones."

"You wouldn't think so, but you'd be surprised. It's tough, and I'm not sure what the solution is." She lifted her shoulder. Then she sighed. "I know for me, it took a little bit of time for me to figure out how to make the different coffees. Since I don't drink my coffee anything but black, it was kind of unfamiliar territory, but the directions are right there. All you have to do is read them and follow them. And that seems to be too hard for some people."

"Maybe it's a reading problem?" he asked, only being half serious.

She recognized that right away and laughed. "You know what, it could possibly be. Maybe I should suggest to Sunny that she should have the directions on audio. Her employees would just have to push a button to have the directions read to them on how to make it."

"Something tells me that the customer wouldn't enjoy that experience quite as much."

"It would ruin the suspense, right?"

They laughed together, and then he said, "Do you want me to take you upstairs? I can show you which bedrooms we've chosen, and then you can decide what you want?"

"Sure. I'll take whatever. I can carry a load of things up with me. I honestly just have pillows and some sheets, and I do have a stand that was my grandmother's that I took with me as well."

"I remember it. I missed it from the library. It was between the two chairs."

"Yeah. I'm kinda surprised you noticed it."

"I thought it was an antique, and it was pretty."

She smiled, and he could tell that his words pleased her. He hadn't realized it was her grandmother's, but that made sense to him now.

"If you don't mind, I think I'll run out to the truck and grab something, and that will halve the time we have to spend carrying stuff in."

"I appreciate it. Actually, you can carry the stand in if you'd like. It's pretty, but it's also very heavy."

"Sure thing. It is in the back?"

"Yeah. Right up next to the cab so the trailer didn't knock it over while I was driving."

"I saw you brought it and unhooked it by the barn. Where'd you have it?"

"I parked it in the pool parking lot. It's closed for the season, and Mrs. Tucker told me it was okay."

"Mrs. Tucker has her fingers in everything," he said, and then as he walked to the back of the truck and she opened the door to grab some things, he said, "I was flabbergasted yesterday in church when she asked me to show some stranger around town."

Summer didn't answer right away, and when she pulled back out of the truck, she had her hands full of several bags of clothes. She closed the door with her arm and shrugged a shoulder. "But it was nice of you to say yes. After all, Mrs. Tucker can be a little bit overbearing, but it takes people like her to keep the town running so well. If she wasn't running around asking people to do things, our town wouldn't have the good reputation that it has as being friendly and helpful, and goodness, the festival wouldn't get done, and one or two people would end up doing everything and then burn out so fast it wouldn't be funny."

They started walking toward the door, and she was right. That stand was extremely heavy.

"This thing looks like solid wood, but I think it might be filled with rocks."

Her laugh rang out. "Right? I had to stop three times while I was carrying it out just to sit down and take a break. My goodness, it's like carrying a little whale around."

"I think a whale would be lighter," he said, opening the door, and she caught it with her foot, holding it with her arm while he used both hands to carry the stand in.

"Thanks," he said, liking the way they worked together. They... had the same vibes that they had had at the festival. Just an easygoing companionship between them that made him feel happy and satisfied.

He carried the stand through the kitchen, down the hall, and into the library, and when he came out, she was waiting at the bottom of the steps.

"You can go up," he said.

"I didn't want to look without you. It...feels familiar, but not. Does that make sense?"

"I suppose. It's kind of got our stamp on it, and that probably feels weird."

"It does."

"I suppose it's hard," he said as he started slowly upstairs. He held his hand out for one of the bags, and she handed it over.

"Not really. I was talking to someone, and they said that I needed to focus on the good, and at first, I thought that was weird because what good is there? I left my home, right? And now I'm a stranger in a home that I used to own."

"I'm sorry."

She shook her head, then stuck her arm back underneath the bag. "Don't be. I promise. It's okay. They pointed out that I don't have any of the worries that I used to have and I get to live here worry free. I pretty much have the best of both worlds. And yeah, I can see some bad things about that, but it just seems silly to focus on the bad."

"That's really wise."

"Yeah. That's what I thought. I was kind of embarrassed that I hadn't thought about it myself. Although, I do think sometimes we can take that to the other extreme and we can totally bury our heads in the sand and we just ignore the things that are wrong. I don't recommend that either. But in my case, I can't do anything about it."

"I see what you're saying. If we can change it, to ignore it is silly and foolish. Or if we should change it."

"Exactly. Like something that's dangerous, or if I want something and I need to work for it. I can't just sit around and think, oh, I'm just going to be happy that I don't have it. No. I can go work for this thing. So, you need a little bit of common sense, but in this case, there was absolutely nothing I could do. I just needed to adjust my attitude so that I was happy instead of wallowing in self-pity."

"It's too bad that more people don't think like that. I think we'd all be happier. But instead, we focus on the bad, on what we don't have, on what wasn't given to us, on how people didn't treat us right, or on how we feel like we're the victim. You know, when you're the victim, you become powerless. I don't understand why it's so popular to pretend to be a victim anymore."

"That's sad, in a way. A lot of people are being convinced that they're victims, and that someone else needs to do something in order for them to be justified. But in reality, you're only as much of a victim as you allow yourself to be. I mean, I could say I was a victim of my parents' overspending, but in reality, I'd rather look at it like I was able to build my own life. I was given the opportunity to learn how hard it is to make things work, how freeing it can be to let things go. And now, I owe nothing, and I'm able to start building my life from the bottom up. It was actually a blessing."

"If that's how you choose to look at it. Which I think is the smart way. But so many people choose to look at themselves as victims and reject the idea that they might be able to do something with what they've been given. Instead, they're looking around and demanding that they be compensated for the unfairness of society."

They had reached the top of the steps, and she looked around. "Which rooms are taken?"

Chapter Eighteen

*E*verything really did look different. It was tough to not feel a little bit of sadness at how it used to be. But the changes weren't bad. In fact, she truly was happy that the house had children in it again and was housing a family. Helping a family heal from a terrible tragedy. Although, when he had talked about his wife at the festival, he didn't really say anything about her sickness or her death. Or how he felt about it. Maybe it was obvious. Of course he was sad, but...there was something that seemed a little off, and she felt like there was maybe more to the story.

He pointed out the three bedrooms that his children had claimed and then pointed at the end of the hall where his bedroom was.

"That was my old bedroom," she said with a smile.

He nodded, and she wondered if he had chosen that on purpose.

No. That was ridiculous. Except, he would have known which bedroom was hers because it was the only one that truly looked lived in when he had gone through the house with the realtor. But he was a man. Did men really notice those things? No. Surely not.

But she didn't know why he would have chosen that room. It didn't have a bathroom connected to it, and it was the smallest of all the six rooms, since the new bathroom that her mother had put in had taken some of the room from that bedroom.

"All right. I guess I'll take this room," she said, pointing at a room that had been empty the entire time she'd been growing up. It had a beautiful view of the backyard, and she always really liked it because it got the morning and afternoon sun, sitting on the corner the way it did. It didn't have a bathroom though, which possibly was the reason his children didn't choose it.

The room that her parents had shared had been taken by Larissa, and that made her smile. It was the largest room and had a huge, massive bath, a jack and jill sink, and a tile shower as well as a separate clawfoot tub.

She had loved that bathroom, and occasionally after her parents had passed, she had soaked in the tub.

"All right then. I'll help you carry the rest of your stuff up. Does it all go up here?"

"I have the plants that you specifically requested," she said with a grin.

"I can't believe how much of a difference they make in the kitchen. I was so disappointed when I got in the kitchen and realized that you'd taken the plants with you. You'd left so many other things."

"I should have said something. But either I was going to hire a mover to move them into a storage facility, or I was going to let you do it. Because after all, Sunny certainly couldn't handle all that in her small apartment above the bakery."

"I had figured as much." He laughed. "I thought that if you could take anything with you, you'd have taken the horses and then fit them in that tiny apartment before you took that furniture in that formal living room."

"Doesn't it look so uncomfortable?" she said with a shudder.

"Oh my goodness, yes. Uncomfortable, and it looks like I'm going to break it if I sit down in it."

"I'll let you know a little secret though. Two of the chairs beside the windows are recliners, and they are much more comfortable, and sturdy, than what they look. You can trust me on that."

"I didn't think anyone had ever been in that room. It looked undisturbed. Like King Tut's tomb or something."

They laughed as they walked outside, and she realized she was having a great time with him. They chatted some more as they carried the rest of the stuff up, and then he said, "I made pancakes for breakfast this morning, and I doubled the recipe but didn't put them all on. Would you like me to cook a couple before we go out to do the fence?"

"Hang on a second. I'll bring in the scones that I brought from the bakeshop, and we'll have those and the pancakes as a little brunch."

He grinned at her, and she ran out to the truck. She'd forgotten about the bag that she'd left on the front seat. For some reason, she had wanted to go in and make sure that everything was still kosher. It just felt like too good to be true, and he might have changed his mind between when they talked at the festival and this morning, even though she'd seen him in church and he was still on board with everything.

Chapter Nineteen

By the time Summer got back in, Gilbert had the griddle out and had poured batter onto it.

"There's a chocolate and a strawberry. Do you have a preference?"

"I'm happy with either," he said, glancing up from the griddle before looking back down and making sure that he poured the batter carefully.

"All right. I love them both too, but I'm partial to chocolate, so I'll give you the strawberry, unless you hate it."

"I love strawberry. I'd probably choose fruit over chocolate, although I know that that's a bit of a controversial subject. And I could probably go to jail for that if I was in the presence of the wrong person when I said it."

"I'm not going to send you to jail, but I am going to wonder a little bit about your sanity. Preferring fruit over chocolate? Now, chocolate-covered fruit? I can totally get that."

"It's like the best of both worlds?"

"Yep. Although, honestly, I prefer caramel and chocolate. Healthy stuff is wonderful, but if you can have a double shot of unhealthy, why not, right?" She looked over her shoulder, and they laughed together.

She knew she had left some paper plates in the pantry, so she felt a little conspicuous as she walked over, but if he truly wanted her to make herself at home, she couldn't keep asking him if she could go places. So, she opened the pantry door, walked in, and saw that it was almost as empty and bare as it was when she moved out. Grabbing paper plates, she walked back out.

"Looks like you didn't have a whole lot of kitchen stuff either."

"I had some at our old house. I guess I should say Desire had some. But I didn't move all that stuff when I sold the house. I did what you did, just left a good bit of it there for the next owners to either use or deal with."

"I'm sorry. It was probably really hard with your wife and everything."

He lifted his shoulder, almost as though he was saying it wasn't that bad, but she didn't question him, because he continued speaking. "We were moving into Mom's house, and I didn't want to bring all of my stuff there. I felt a little bit wasteful, because we were struggling for money at the time, and a yard sale would have brought in a good bit of cash. I just didn't have the brainpower or the energy level to do that. I was trying to run the business, trying to figure out why it was losing money all of a sudden, trying to run my wife from appointment to appointment, and trying to keep up with the kids and not burden my mom any more than I had to."

"That sounds like a really black, hard time."

"I think it's a little bit like what we were talking about before, where it was a hard time, but I learned a lot of good lessons."

"Such as?" she prompted, getting silverware out of the drawer and setting it beside the paper plates before grabbing glasses and filling them up with water from the tap.

"Such as I was afraid to be a parent without my wife. She was the one who took care of almost everything with the kids. And when she wasn't around, I... I guess I wondered if I could do it. Find shoes before school, get the kids breakfast, and get them on the bus without having a nuclear meltdown—that would be me, not them, and that's a good thing. It just felt overwhelming."

"Because you were dumped into it."

"Yeah."

"And you had your business to deal with, too. When she was doing it, she wasn't trying to figure out what was wrong with the business and care for a spouse with cancer."

"Good point." He grinned up at her before flipping the pancakes.

"You look like you're pretty good at that. So I guess that's one of the things you learned, is how to cook."

"Oh, I already knew that. Mom made sure that we all learned to cook before we left the house. I guess she heard horror stories of children who left home and couldn't take care of themselves, to the point where they couldn't feed themselves or even know how to wash their own clothes."

"Wow. I can't imagine serving your children to the point where they can't do anything for themselves."

"I know, right? Although kids spend so much time at school nowadays and then after school at sports and extracurricular activities that they really don't have time to learn how to do those things. Or, I guess more accurately, if you're going to teach them how to do those things, you have to be very deliberate about it, because you're not going to be able to just make it happen, most likely."

"That's a good point. I guess I don't have children, so that's not really something that I understand, other than I know that equine therapy is something that takes kids away from the home and keeps them from having time to do those chores." She smiled and made sure that her gaze was understanding as he looked up with a guilty look.

"I wasn't accusing you of anything."

"I know. We just are coming at it from completely different perspectives. Since I've never had kids, and I don't really know what it's like."

"Well, you'll be living with three, so you might have your eyes opened in a few ways that you weren't expecting."

"And I think that's good."

"Yeah." He slipped the pancakes off the griddle and put two on her plate and two on his. "Think you'll eat twice as much as that?"

"I didn't have any breakfast this morning, so if you cook it, I'll probably eat it."

"All right. Let me put four more on here, and then I'll say grace."

He was going to say grace. That was not good for her heart, which seemed to be beating super hard in her chest, and the feeling of attraction just seemed to be amplified. She watched as his hands held the spatula, and he moved about the kitchen like he knew what he was doing. It was obvious that he wasn't making it up, that he truly did know his way around the kitchen, and that he truly had learned to cook.

Of course, she knew that Larissa had learned as well and that teaching his kids the essentials of life seemed to be important to him.

She just admired and respected so much about him, and felt comfortable with him in a way that surprised her. Especially since their interactions at church yesterday had been awkward. But maybe that had been her, because she hadn't known how to act now that she knew that she was going to be living here.

He set two more pancakes on her plate and then set two more on his before setting the butter and the syrup down in front of them and taking his seat.

"Ready?" he asked, lifting a brow as she nodded.

He bowed his head and said a simple prayer as she listened, thanking God that she'd met him. Whatever it was, she admired him, and even if this Darla person really was perfect for him, and... that would be awkward. She hadn't even considered that. What if he and Darla got serious, and—

"Amen," he said, in such a way that she could tell he was saying it for the second time.

"Oh my goodness. I am so sorry. But I had a thought while we were praying that kind of shocked me."

"Yeah?" he asked, and she could tell he was interested.

"Okay. Hear me out. Because I haven't thought about this much, since it just occurred to me just now."

"All right."

"What if you and Darla, or you and someone else, get serious. And you get married. I...live here in your house. What is your wife going to think about that?"

He had already shoved a bite of pancakes in his mouth, and he lifted a shoulder, like it didn't matter, before he chewed and swallowed. "We'll deal with it. We'll figure it out. Whoever it is, whatever she is, she's going to have to understand that I gave my word to you, and that's the way it's going to be."

He speared two more pieces of pancake, dipping them in syrup and then holding them up before he said, "I did hear from someone that it might be a little bit...not good for the town to look at us and see that we're quote, unquote, living together?" He made it sound like a bit of a question. He held his pancakes steady and didn't put them in his mouth, as though he wanted to make sure he saw her reaction.

"Does that bother you?" she asked, running that over in her head. She definitely had thought of that, but just in passing.

"I don't know. I know we want to avoid all appearance of evil, but at the same time, there's no evil going on here. It's just me giving you a place to stay so that you can continue to run your equine counseling business from this farm. I guess I look at it as a good deed. And honestly as I was thinking about it this morning, I just had a sense of peace about it. Like this was all part of God's plan. I certainly didn't buy the farm thinking that you were going to stay here, and I was actually kind of castigating myself because I didn't help you stay on the farm, instead of trying to buy it for myself."

"We're not socialist here. You're not supposed to try to help everyone else at the expense of yourself."

"No. But I'm a Christian. Christianity is an individual thing, socialism is something that's forced on a society by their government. I definitely do not believe in socialism at all. The government doesn't have the right to tell citizens what they may and may not buy or what they may or may not have, or to institute controls regarding those things. However, me as an individual is completely different."

"But it sounds to me like you feel comfortable that you're doing what God wants you to do, and I told you, you lifted the burden of stress and worry off my shoulders and have given me the best of both worlds. I think it's turned out perfectly. By the way, these pancakes are amazing," she said, waving her fork around before she put it in her mouth.

"Thank you. The kids didn't seem to have any trouble eating them, but they didn't tell me that they tasted okay. So I was left wondering if they're just bottomless pits, or whether the pancakes just tasted that good."

"I can't really speak to the anatomy of your children's stomachs, however, I do believe it's a genetic thing, so perhaps you can think about your own stomach and answer that question without my help. As for me, the pancakes are amazing."

He smiled and nodded, and they ate a little bit more.

"I guess, now that you brought it up, if there comes a point where I get serious about someone, I'll have to talk to them about you. Because you're here. And I'm not making you go anywhere. The offer stands."

"Well, we did say that you would give me two months' notice if I had to vacate the premises. It makes sense that if you get married, your wife probably wouldn't appreciate having me around. So maybe I can just plan on moving out if you get married." It would be awkward to stay. Especially with the way she was fighting her feelings. He obviously was completely oblivious, but the idea of getting married to someone else was something that he was considering.

Something told her that she wasn't going to be able to stay here if he was with someone else. Maybe it was a woman's intuition, or maybe it was just her being realistic, but regardless, she was almost one-hundred-percent sure that was true.

"Maybe by the time I find someone, we can have the apartment over the stable finished, and that might be an option as well."

"Possibly," she said, and she maybe would be able to do that. If she lived above the stable, she wouldn't have to come to the house at all, although it would be hard to see Gilbert with someone else, enjoying his family and being affectionate with another woman.

She was an adult though. She could handle it.

She wanted to think that, but she wasn't entirely sure it was true.

They finished the pancakes, gobbled down the scones, and got up to do the dishes themselves.

The trash was where she always had it, in the most obvious place between the sink and the refrigerator.

It was funny how things changed but didn't.

"It looks like we're going to have another gorgeous fall day, which probably is the best time for fixing fence."

"I agree. I've fixed fence in some inclement weather, and it's not fun at all. In fact, the last time I did it, I'm pretty sure I smashed my thumb and lost my nail over it."

"Ouch."

"Yeah. It's the hazards of the job, I suppose."

They finished up the dishes and walked out together, with Summer feeling torn. On the one hand, she was having a great time and possibly falling in love with this man who didn't seem to notice her in that way at all. Maybe their discussion about how much older he was than her, and how she didn't have any children and was from a different age group, who couldn't understand people who did have kids, had made him decide she wasn't worth looking at.

Regardless, that feeling was tempered with the enjoyment she felt being with him.

Chapter Twenty

"And then the mother told me that it was the father who needed the therapy, not the kids!" Summer ended her story, and Gilbert barked out a laugh.

She was funny, she knew how to poke fun at herself, and she didn't mind him laughing at her too.

They'd fixed eight or nine places in the fence that needed some attention, and together they were walking back through the far end of the pasture toward the house.

He wanted to find a few more holes in the fence to fix, but as much as he searched, he couldn't find anything. He just wanted their time together to never end.

"I really appreciate you coming out with me today."

"Of course. I appreciate you telling me that you were doing it. After all, it's my horses that are going to benefit."

"That might be true, but—"

"If you're even going to say something about me giving your kids therapy without charging you, I don't want to hear it. You said that so much already, and it really wasn't that big of a deal. I told you, I had an affinity toward your kids, and especially Larissa. I just want to see them succeed."

"I think that's what you want with everyone. You are selfless, in the very best way, and I admire that. I'd like to be more like that."

"I'd like to be more like that too. You make me sound better than what I am."

"No, I don't think so, and trust me, I know what selfishness looks like. My wife—" He stopped abruptly. He hadn't meant to talk about Desire. He didn't want to ruin the day.

"I'm sure those memories are painful for you," Summer said, all traces of a smile off her face and concern and sadness replacing it.

He hated that she was deceived. She didn't understand that it certainly wasn't sadness or pain that kept him from talking.

"She cheated on me." There, the words were out. It felt good to say them.

Summer's eyes widened, and she stopped walking, planting the stick that she used as a walking stick in the ground. "What? I've never heard anything about that around town. Not that I listen to a whole lot of gossip, but that's definitely something that would have made the rounds."

"It certainly would have. But I never said it."

"Oh. All right. Well, you can rest assured that I won't say anything."

"I knew you wouldn't. I guess that's why I felt safe saying it. You can't begin to imagine how good that felt."

"Yeah. Why in the world would you keep that to yourself?"

"My kids. I didn't want them to think badly about their mother."

"It's one thing to think badly about their mother because you're smearing her, trying to make her look bad. It's another thing to speak the truth about her." Summer still sounded like she couldn't quite believe either that his wife cheated or that he hadn't told his kids. He wasn't sure which.

"But she's not here. She can't defend herself, although she admitted to me that she had been cheating."

"That's devastating," she said, immediately getting to the word that best described how he felt.

"Yeah. We'd… We'd been together for so long, and I eventually found out that the time I discovered wasn't the first time."

"Oh no." She put her hand over her mouth.

"Yeah. I'm sorry, I kind of feel like I'm dumping on you, but I hadn't told anyone. I didn't want people to know. I guess part of it's because I'm so embarrassed. What kind of man am I that I couldn't even keep my wife?"

"It's not your fault that she doesn't have character."

"I know those words are true, but it's hard to apply that to yourself when it's your spouse that doesn't stay true to you. You wonder what's wrong with you? What did you do? What didn't you do? How could you have prevented this?"

"It's not on you. It's on them. It shouldn't matter how terrible you are, if they can't keep their word, if they can't keep their eyes on themselves, if they don't have the character to do right, it's not your fault."

"Yes, I know what you're saying is true, but—"

"Okay. I believe you. I suppose it would be devastating in a way, but I guess I would be angry."

"Oh, trust me. There were plenty of times where I was angry," he said, holding a two-by-four braced against the ground as he stood and stared at her. He couldn't believe he had admitted to her something he hadn't admitted to anyone, not his mother or sisters, or his best friends. But she just felt so safe.

"It was tough when she died. Because of course the kids were sad, and that was the thing that ripped my heart. Because I had trouble feeling anything. Other than a faint sense of relief and a little bit of wonderment about whether or not that might be God's punishment for her."

"I guess it could be. I hate to think that that's what God does, although in the Old Testament, He certainly did punish people that way."

"I know. And he is the same God yesterday, today, and forever, but we're living in the dispensation of grace. Which I need, even more than she did maybe. Because like I said, I was angry. I didn't think about killing her, but I did wish she would die. So then I felt guilty when she got cancer. Was that my fault? Did I wish that upon her?"

"If wishes were horses, beggars would drive," she said, repeating the little ditty that he hadn't heard in a long time.

"I suppose that's true, but it's still tough. I... I guess we kind of came to a mutual understanding, but I always wondered, and I wonder now a lot, if she hadn't died, would we still be together? Because I was determined that if she cheated on me again, I wasn't going to stay. Or maybe more accurately, I wasn't going to allow her to stay. But she didn't seem to be able to help herself."

"I've heard that. Like serial cheaters who really, truly love the person that they're with, but just... I don't know if they get bored exactly, or if they just can't stay true to one person."

"Yeah, part of me wonders if she could help it, and then another part of me thinks about the times that I intend to do wrong, want to do wrong, and I don't. I'd like to be able to say I can't help it, but I do? So couldn't she?"

"That's a good point. Why do some people seem to be incapable of resisting temptation, and seem to thrive on doing whatever they want, and then just issue an apology like that will make it all go away. It doesn't really seem fair or right."

"Exactly."

He looked at the ground, the grass green underneath, but brown on top. Typical for November. Maybe if he had been there, they could have gotten another cutting off that and made some hay.

That seemed like an odd thing to think about after he had just told this woman, this woman who seemed to fit him perfectly, about his wife.

"So that was a real struggle then. As she was dying, it would have been hard to see your children so sad. I guess it would have been tempting for me to let them know that they weren't losing as much as they thought they were. And let them know about her character."

"I suppose sometimes I wanted to, but mostly I don't want them to know. I don't want them to think less of her. But at the same time…it's the truth. And I wondered too if it would help them get over her better if I told them that maybe we weren't going to stay together, or if that would rock the foundations of everything that they believed."

"I think that's probably right. And sometimes we have a tendency to attack the messenger. They might turn around and hate you for telling them the truth about their mom. That doesn't make any sense, but sometimes humans don't make any sense."

"Tell me about it," he muttered, and she laughed. He had been being serious, but he supposed it was funny, too.

"Humans really don't make sense sometimes. And I suppose you can't say this, but I can: especially women."

"Amen," he said, and then he laughed too. He liked that she wasn't afraid to poke fun at her gender. And she could say the things that were true or obvious, but things people often didn't want to say because they were too scared.

"I think maybe women have a tendency to run on emotion more than men do. And that's what makes us so illogical. Because we allow our emotions to control us. I've noticed my tendency toward doing that, and I try to curtail that, because while I feel emotion is important, obviously God gave it to us, and it serves an important purpose in our life, it's not what we should allow to direct our day-to-day life. We should do things because they're right, because we're supposed to do them, because we have character and we do the right thing, we choose that, not because we feel like it or don't feel like it."

"It's too bad more people don't feel that way, because you're absolutely right. People run on emotion, and they don't feel like doing it, so they don't. That doesn't get you anywhere."

"It's not right. I mean, I don't necessarily think that we should shove our emotions aside and pretend that we don't have any, but at the same time, we can't allow them to dictate how we live our lives. Otherwise no one would stay true, because there's always going to be a time when you're attracted to someone you shouldn't be attracted to, and how are you going to handle that? Go with your emotions? That's wrong."

"Maybe that was Desire's problem. She had never learned to put what she felt aside and do the right thing."

"Well, she did stay with you. There was that at least."

"She tried to run off with her boyfriend, but he was married too, and he didn't want to leave his wife. He just wanted someone to play with on the side." He looked at his shoulder. "At least that was one of her lovers. There were apparently other ones, and I'm not sure why she didn't run off with any of them. I suppose I could try to dig it all up, but I don't want to, you know?"

"Yeah. I totally get that. Sometimes things are better left in the past. Because they would just upset us and make us angry. And there's really nothing to be done about it now anyway."

"Other than to find out whether or not my children are actually mine," he muttered, then he met her eyes, which widened at his statement. Obviously she hadn't thought that far ahead.

"Oh my goodness." Then she shook her head and flattened her lips. "It wouldn't make any difference at all. You would still love your children as yours, if you found out they weren't. Worse, if somehow that word got out, someone else might try to take them from you, and that would devastate you. So you don't even want to go there." She sounded so sure, so convinced that he was going to do the right thing, that he was shocked for a moment.

"It took me weeks to come to that conclusion."

"But I knew you would right away, because that's the kind of person you are."

"Maybe that's where your intuition works with logic. You come to the right conclusion, where I was just using logic, and it took me a while to think on it."

"Possibly," she said, sounding almost cheerful. Maybe she was happy that she was right. She knew she was living with someone who was a little bit decent.

She didn't seem to look down on him because he couldn't keep his wife true. Even though he knew it wasn't his fault. Even though she had just said that it wasn't his fault, sometimes he still felt like it was. Like he should have done something or been more or somehow been able to keep her attention.

He knew there were people who would say that he wasn't a good husband, and that's why his wife had cheated.

He leaned on the board, allowing it to wobble and maybe lean a little bit as he thought. "I'm sorry I dumped on you."

"No. Honestly, I was curious. But I didn't want to ask. It just seemed too much like prying."

"I thought I told you that you could ask anything you wanted to, and I would be okay with it?"

"Yeah, but I assumed you meant normal questions, not personal questions about stuff that you might not rather tell people. And you did say that you hadn't told anyone."

"True. But you're different." Those words came out before he wanted them to, and as hard as he clamped his teeth together, he couldn't get them to come back in. They sat out there, floating in the air, as he watched her eyes widen as though in slow motion, and expressions flitted across her face, after surprise came thoughtfulness, and then she looked almost happy.

"I appreciate that. I… I feel different with you than I do with other people. And I can't figure out exactly what that is. But you feel safe to me."

He didn't really want to feel safe. Exactly. But maybe safe would lead to something else. Although, he kind of felt like safe was probably a lot like putting him in the friend zone.

"Safe?" he finally said, figuring that if he expected her to ask the questions that she wanted to but was a little afraid to, he should too.

"Just comfortable. Like I can trust you with things I can't trust other people with. I really love being with you. Just because it feels so good."

He grinned, and he wasn't sure whether it was him deliberately taking a step forward, or maybe he lost his balance a little as he held the board on the ground, but he took a step toward her and reached out, putting his hand on her shoulder, maybe to catch his balance or maybe because he needed to touch her.

"It's been a long time since I've wanted to kiss someone, but that's pretty much all I've been thinking about. That, and how much I enjoy spending time with you. I almost wish that there were more holes in the fence so that we can keep working together. And it's not because I love fixing fence so much."

She laughed, but it sounded a little nervous.

"Did you just say you wanted to kiss me?" she asked, and maybe her voice was a little higher.

He nodded, watching her face as the expressions flew across it. It was so expressive. "That, and since the first time I saw you, I wanted to put my fingers in your hair. It is almost something I have to ball my fist up and determine not to do."

"You can do it," she said as she moved her hand up and put it over his, taking it off her shoulder and threading his fingers through her hair. He went down the strands and wrapped them around his fist.

"So soft," he said.

"I didn't know you liked it."

How could she not know? It was like a beacon to him. "Anywhere you are, it just draws my eyes. Maybe that's just because it's part of you." His hand went down, feeling the silky softness as it slid around his fist before he reached the end, and it fell off.

Immediately he brought his hand back up and put it in her hair again.

"Now, about the kiss?" she said, and she didn't sound nearly as confident.

He should say no. He should say they should wait. He should say they needed to talk about it, because she couldn't be living at his house if he were kissing her out in the pasture field. But he didn't say any of those things.

He said, "What about you?"

"Yes," she said, her eyes crinkling and compelling him to laugh along with her.

"I'm not going to look a gift horse in the mouth," he said, causing her to laugh out loud. The sound cut off abruptly as his lips caught hers, and her laugh became a part of him. The board fell to the ground, as he let go of it in order to wrap his other arm around her and bury that hand in her hair as well.

She must have dropped the hammer she carried, and he had no idea what happened to the container of staples in her other hand, since he felt both of her hands wrapping around his back.

He'd kissed his wife plenty of times, but never out in an open pasture field, and never with as much abandon as what he kissed Summer. All thoughts fled, and all he could think about was trying to get closer to her, the silky softness of her hair, and the feel of her lips under his.

He finally tore his lips from hers, but as though unable to completely break contact, he kept his arms wrapped around her and his hands buried in her hair as he moved his lips up across her cheek and along her temple.

"I know we shouldn't have done that. I know I should apologize. But I wanted to, and I'm not sorry."

"Don't apologize, you'll ruin it," she whispered, and he was gratified to hear that she was out of breath, since he felt like he had just run a marathon. His legs were weak, his heart beat fast, and his lungs couldn't get enough air.

"I can't do this," he said. "Not if you're living in my house. I know this. But... This is exactly how I feel. Everything I wanted to do."

"Me too. But you're right. I can't live in your house, if this is what we're going to do every time we're alone."

Chapter Twenty-One

Gilbert took a deep breath and forced his hands to open up, allowing Summer's hair to spill out.

He took a step back.

He sucked another deep breath into his lungs as they stared at each other, her hands falling off him and her eyes searching his.

"I'm sorry, but that was...amazing. Far better than I dreamed it could be, but we won't let it happen again, right?" she said, lifting her brows and looking at him.

"Yeah. It won't happen again. We... We need to set a good example for the kids, and we can't be sneaking off and kissing all the time."

"Even if we want to," she said, making it sound more like a question than a statement.

He nodded. "Even if that's the only thing I can think about all day long, is getting you in my arms, running my hands through your hair, and your lips on mine, we can't."

"Right. I won't think about it either. Although, now I have much more to think about."

"Same. It's one thing to think theoretically, it's another thing to think in concrete terms."

"Yeah."

They stood staring at each other, both of them breathing hard, both of them knowing that what they had just done could not be repeated, and then he wasn't sure whether it was him, whether it was her, but they seemed to move as one, taking a step toward the other and reaching for each other, his lips coming down as hers lifted, and his hands burying again in her hair as she sighed and melted against him.

This kiss was even better than the first, and he didn't even know how that was possible. He was too old to feel things like this. He was in his thirties, for goodness' sake. He wasn't a teenager anymore, but she made him feel all the things he had originally felt with his wife, only deeper and stronger and with substance behind them. Since he knew the kind of person she was, and the things that she did, and the way she lived her life. But she was the kind of person he admired and respected and wouldn't mind spending the rest of his life with.

This time, it was her that pulled away, although her lips ran along his jawline and down his neck as her hands moved over his chest and down his rib cage.

"I shouldn't have done that," she said, her eyes closed, her words pained.

"I shouldn't have let you."

She took a deep breath, and after moving her arms up his chest and down his biceps, she took a deliberate step back. "All right. That was...better than the first one. It makes me wonder if a third might be even more spectacular, but I'm afraid that it would be foolish to try and find out."

He ran a hand through his hair and hooked it around his neck. What was he going to do? He couldn't live in the same house as this woman if he couldn't keep his hands off her. Or, more accurately, his lips.

"Yeah, I was actually just thinking that."

"If we're going to do that again, I think I'm going to need to sit down. That, or I'm going to fall."

"No. Sitting down is way too close to lying down, and that way lies trouble. I don't want our relationship to go that way. We do have a relationship?" He lifted his brows and couldn't help holding his breath.

"Yes. Oh goodness, yes."

He smiled. "That's exactly what I wanted to hear."

They grinned at each other.

"All right. We're going to have to figure this out."

She nodded. "I can move back out. I think it's probably dangerous for me to live here."

"No." The word was said immediately. "If anyone moves out, it'll be me."

"But you own the place, and your kids are here."

"I'm not doing this to play. Maybe I should have said that to begin with, although I wasn't expecting to kiss you today. I... I'm not messing around."

"I'm not either," she said, looking confused.

"I mean, I want to court you. I want to get married. I'm not asking you right now, but I don't kiss just anyone. And definitely I don't do it to you."

"I see what you're saying. I think kissing should be mostly between married people. I just haven't been acting that way for the last fifteen minutes."

"Me either. But that's what I believe as well. So... It's not going to be long until I ask you to be my wife. But it seems a little soon right now."

"Okay," she said, seeming to be processing what he was saying and keeping up, although she still looked a little dazed, and her lips were definitely swollen. She looked beautiful to him, and he resisted the urge to kiss her again.

"So, I have some thoughts. Do you want to hear them?"

"Sure. I guess I don't have any thoughts right now." She rolled her eyes and laughed a little, and he wanted to reach out to put his hand on her shoulder, to tell her that he understood. But he did think it was better to not touch her.

"All right, I guess I just might as well be up front and say it's better if I don't touch you."

"I agree. I think that's probably where we went wrong. If you have that guard in place, you're certainly not going to do anything else that you shouldn't be doing."

"Exactly. So, no touching, then I don't have to say no kissing or anything else."

"Right. I'll try to control myself, and you seem to have plenty of self-control—"

"No. I'll have to work on controlling myself as well. I think making sure that the children are around as long as they're home is probably a good idea."

"Yes. That's a good idea."

"And learning as much as we can about each other, so that we're sure this is the right way to go, is probably another good idea."

"I always thought the best way to learn about someone was to work with them. When you do that, you know how they respond to situations that don't go their way."

"I agree. Just living life. Like if you could see me this morning when I burned the pancakes and broke the measuring cup, you would see how I act when I'm under pressure."

"Yeah. I guess you see me when I'm working with my clients, but you didn't see me crying in my house when I knew I was going to have to sell my horses."

"I'd rather you sit and cry than stomp around and break stuff."

"I didn't do that, but I guess maybe I was a little tempted to."

"I can imagine."

"Well, I think we all have those sides of our personality that we hope don't come out or see the light of day."

"For some reason, that reminds me that my family was hoping that we could have Thanksgiving here at our house."

"Of course. Do you need me to leave for the day?" she asked, and while she looked like she was willing to do it, he thought there might have been a little bit of hurt in her undertone.

"No!" He shook his head. "No. I was thinking that maybe... Maybe I could tell them that you and I are..." He shrugged and laughed. What was he going to say? How would he describe them? "I don't know what to call us."

"That we're together?"

"That I'm hoping we'll be married before Christmas?" he countered.

"Before Christmas?" She blinked.

"I told you I wasn't missing round. I don't want to push you. If you think that's too soon. I don't trust my self-control, and I also don't know how wise it is for us to be living together if we're together. People are going to talk. And the shorter that amount of time is, the better."

Already she was nodding in agreement. "I see, and I agree. Definitely we can tell your family that we're together and hope to be married before Christmas."

"That's not too soon?"

"It might take a little getting used to, but we can tell your family, and maybe we can ask them to just keep it under their hats for a bit?"

"My family will do that. My mom is the one who really talks to people, but she doesn't spread gossip about her children, and I know she definitely won't if I ask her specifically not to."

"All right then. Let's do it."

"I'll help you with the meal. I'm not expecting you to cook it all by yourself, and I'm not expecting you to be by yourself either."

"I don't mind. I've never gotten to cook a Thanksgiving meal for a big family like that. I've actually always dreamed about having a big family on Christmas. So Thanksgiving is kind of a dream come true. Almost."

He laughed. "I guess you could ask them if they'd like to come on Christmas too, just so they can make your dreams come true."

"That's really sweet." She looked like she wanted to close the distance between them and put her arms around him, and he knew that if she did that, he wasn't going to be able to step away from her. Because he was fighting the urge to do the same.

"All right, then we'll try to work together, and spend time together, but not alone, and that'll be easy because the kids have school off starting Wednesday and they're off until Tuesday of next week."

"All right. We won't have to worry about anything until next Tuesday. And after that, maybe I'll be working with my clients during the day."

"And I can focus on doing some other repairs around the place. I noticed that the basement was starting to be finished, but it looked like someone stopped in the middle of it."

"That's where my mom ran out of money for the last time."

"I have a little bit of extra, and maybe I'll work on that. It'll be a nice place for the kids to play in the winter when it's not nice enough to go outside."

"That sounds like a good idea. I'm sure they would enjoy that."

"So, I guess I don't need to point out to you that this old man comes with three kids."

"You're not an old man, and I think that's an asset. Not a liability."

"I think that's what makes you special. Because most women wouldn't see it that way."

"I do. For sure."

"Do you want children of your own?" he asked softly, knowing that it didn't matter either way to him. Although, the more time he spent with her, the more he wouldn't mind raising a child with her. One with her eyes and her heart-shaped face.

"I used to. But... I don't want you to have to start all over. That maybe seems a little discouraging. And you've been at this raising kids thing for a while. Maybe you're ready to be done."

"I guess you can keep thinking about it. Because if you'd like kids, I'm fine with that, but I guess I'm not desperate to have more."

She nodded, and he thought that she would be honest with him and tell him if she really felt strongly one way or the other. He had been absolutely honest in telling her that he didn't care. Although, he supposed he was leaning a little bit more toward not. Which wasn't very romantic, but she was right, he'd been doing it for a while, and he knew how much time small children took. He'd like to be able to just spend time with Summer and not have children between them.

"Maybe we can adopt," Summer said suddenly as she bent to pick up the box of staples that she dropped.

"Yeah. I guess I never thought about that, but I'd be okay with that."

"We could be foster parents. That way, we have children, but maybe not all the time, as they come and go in our house."

"That's a good idea."

"I wouldn't want your children to be put out, if we did that."

"We could talk to them and see how they feel about it, but I kind of feel like they might be excited about sharing their home with other kids."

"I thought that's the way they'd feel too. They have such big hearts. Maybe that comes with losing their mom, but they're very empathetic."

"Thank you," he said, bending over and picking up the board.

He hadn't meant to kiss her, hadn't meant to lose control of himself the way he had, but he thought that maybe it worked out. They'd set some boundaries, and if they could stick with them, maybe they could develop the kind of relationship that wasn't based on physical attraction, although that was obviously between them, but based on biblical love and character. After all, he'd been married to someone who didn't have that kind of character, and he didn't want to make that mistake again. While he was almost certain he wasn't going to be making it with Summer, she didn't know for sure about him. At least, he assumed she didn't. Maybe she saw things that he didn't know about.

As they walked slowly back to the house, he thought about those things but decided that maybe they should focus more on the practical stuff, and those other things would take care of themselves.

"Do you want me to do the grocery shopping for Thursday?"

"I can do it. Is there anything that your family always has that I need to make sure I get? Or is turkey and mashed potatoes and gravy—the traditional meal—what they're expecting?"

"My sister always makes stuffing balls. That's Amy. Maybe I can give you her number, and she can let you know what the recipe is. I think that's pretty much the only thing that would cause a mutiny if it's not on the table."

"All right. As much as I'm curious as to how you react when your family mutinies, I would prefer not to have it on Thanksgiving. So give me Amy's number, and I'll text her."

He laughed, loving that she was willing to be humble enough to do what his family was used to.

He sent her a text with Amy's number and then said, "I'm not going to be here tomorrow for a while, because I have that thing that Mrs. Tucker asked me to do, but otherwise, I'll be here when your horses get here, in case you have something else planned."

"I should be here all week, other than tomorrow while I'm helping Sunny." Her face got a little cloudy, and he wasn't quite sure what was wrong. "But if I realize that I have to be out, I'll text you, and I appreciate your offer. I know that horses are not people, and I try to keep them in their proper place, but it was pretty devastating to have to let them go, and I'm excited about them coming back."

"It makes me happy to see you happy." Maybe that was how he knew for sure that the direction he was going with Summer was the right one. When his heart got so happy it could burst, just to see her smile, it was a pretty good indication that she meant a lot to him.

Chapter Twenty-Two

"Okay, I think you guys are the cutest ever, but...do you think you're moving too fast?" Sunny looked up from the batter she stirred, her eyes concerned as they met Summer's.

Her chest tightened, and there was a sinking feeling in her stomach.

"I know it is fast. And I don't know what to say about that. Don't some people believe in love at first sight?"

"Sure, love at first sight, but not marriage the day after you decide you're in love. Just because you said I love you to each other doesn't mean you should get married right away."

They hadn't even said that. They just agreed that they were both...attracted to each other? Couldn't keep their lips off each other? Neither one of those things seemed to be the ideal way to counter the idea that they hadn't said I love you, so Summer just kept her eyes on the flour that she was measuring.

"Summer? You're not mad because I told you the truth, are you?"

"No. Not at all. I appreciate you being honest with me, and I figure that's probably the way a lot of people are going to feel. After all, you're not wrong. It's been really fast."

"Yeah. It's going to be surprising, and people are going to talk."

"People are going to talk because I'm living in his house."

Sunny waved a hand in the air. "Everybody does that nowadays. No one thinks a thing about it."

"Christians do. It's not right."

"Christians live together too. In fact, I think Christians live together as much as secular people. The idea of sin is kind of old-fashioned."

"It's not. It's just as relevant today as it ever has been," Summer said, unable to keep the shock and defensiveness out of her tone. She had no idea Sunny felt that way.

"I'm not going to argue with you about it, because you can use the Bible to back up your position, and I know there's no Bible for mine, but that's the way society feels. That if you don't sleep with your boyfriend, if you don't kiss while you're dating, you're being a prude. Everybody does it. I mean, come on, don't they? Do you know a single person who says that it's not okay to kiss whoever you feel like kissing, even a perfect stranger?" Sunny paused. "But everyone, and I mean everyone, will tell you that getting married weeks after you decide you like each other is crazy. I mean, you're not even dating!"

Summer was quiet. It was true that it was hard to find anyone who thought that kissing should be reserved for the person you were getting married to. Even Christians didn't believe like that. A good night kiss after a date was kind of a given. Not that she had had a whole lot of those, but she had two serious relationships, and she knew, from both of them, that the kiss was almost a requirement.

"Never mind about that. I just feel like it's fast. I mean, nobody moves that fast."

"But I thought we just agreed that I'm not doing things the way society does them. I want to live by the Bible. The Bible doesn't say that you can't meet someone one day and get married the next. It just says that the person you marry has to be a believer. And then, after you're married, you have certain requirements you have to meet, and certain things you have to do as husband and wife. So I guess, making sure that the person you're with is a Christian, and then making sure that you're married to someone who is going to uphold their part. You take that seriously, and I feel that Gilbert is that kind of person."

"You would be the first person to tell me that I shouldn't do everything my feelings tell me to do, so why should you? Am I wrong?"

"No. You're exactly right."

"All right then, it doesn't really matter how it feels then, right?"

"No. What I said before is what matters, that he's an upright man, who will do what he says he's going to do, and if he says he's going to stay with me for the rest of my life, I need to believe that."

"I guess you're right. So do you?"

"He hasn't said it, but yes." She thought about the cheating that his wife had done on him and how that had hurt and affected him. He hadn't gone into the pain he felt, but it had been evident in his voice and in his expression. She wasn't going to tell Sunny about it. She couldn't. She said she wasn't going to. "I just know that when he says it, he means it. I can see that. I can see the character in him, and other people can too."

"You mean the character of that man?" Sunny said as she pointed out the window.

Summer had been ready to take her apron off, finished for the day, when Sunny had pointed.

Sure enough, she was absolutely right. It was Gilbert who sat outside across from the bakeshop, on a park bench with another woman.

It must be the Darla that Mrs. Tucker had asked him to spend the day with. She wore high heels, along with slim dress pants, and a fashionable sweater. Her makeup appeared to be applied perfectly from this distance, and her hair was short and stylish, bobbed around her head in a flattering way.

As Summer looked, Darla laughed at something Gilbert said,

throwing her head back and lifting a hand, the bracelet on her wrist sparkling in the sunlight as her rings glittered.

"Yeah. That's the man." She tried to infuse nonchalance to hide the depression that had stolen over her. Appearances could be deceiving. She felt she had to defend him, but she didn't want to sound defensive, because Summer would see right through that. "I was with him Sunday in church when Mrs. Tucker asked him to take someone who is looking to purchase a weekend getaway here in town on a tour."

"Another Washington, DC person looking to get out of the city for the weekend?" Sunny rolled her eyes. They were nice for the money, but their beliefs contrasted with those of most small-town residents, and they tended to be loud and vocal, and ordinances and rules were changed to accommodate them.

They were not popular with the locals.

"Yes. She sounded really nice," Summer offered.

"I'm sure she did. She looks like a DC suit. And your boyfriend looks like he's having a really good time with her."

"He's not really my boyfriend, and I was telling you, Mrs. Tucker asked him to show her around. He said he would. And... He's doing what he said."

"Let me get this straight. Yesterday he was kissing you, today he's all snuggled up with her on the park bench."

"No. They're not snuggled up." They weren't even touching, although she had her body pointed toward him, and as she spoke, she put a hand on his knee.

Even from this distance, Summer could see that he was uncomfortable with it as he moved around, pretty much doing everything but picking up her hand and taking it off his leg.

Or maybe that was what she wanted him to be doing. Maybe he actually enjoyed her hand being there. Maybe he'd realize that a businesswoman was exactly what he wanted, as she had been afraid of on Sunday when she had heard Mrs. Tucker ask him to spend time with Darla.

"I'm sorry. I don't need to rub it in." Sunny's arm came around her shoulder, and her voice sounded sincere and compassionate.

"It's okay. I really think that he's just doing what Mrs. Tucker asked. But... It doesn't feel good."

"But we don't go by our feelings, right?"

"That's right. I can't react in a negative way just because I don't like what I see. I actually do appreciate the character of a man who does what he says he's going to do, even if he doesn't want to."

"Even though it looks like he's having a good time, probably, deep down, he doesn't want to," Sunny said, and Summer did not miss the sarcasm in her voice.

"Right. That's exactly what I want to hear, but—"

"It's not necessarily the truth. I don't know, Summer. I really want this to be good for you, but I've played devil's advocate a little bit because I don't want to see you hurt. You're special. You are one of the best humans I know. And you have a tendency to trust everyone. You just believe them. But sometimes that bites you. Sometimes your gullibility hurts. And this is a pretty big decision. Now, you're right, he is a Christian, and I like the fact that both of you have decided to not touch. I agree with that, even though I told you that no one else does it. That's true, but if you have that kind of self-control, that's the best way to be."

Summer listened, but she watched out the window as Darla laughed again, and Gilbert smiled. He had a smile that she absolutely loved. And forgive her, but she had thought that it was only for her. Obviously it was a smile he used on everyone. He didn't seem like he was fighting the urge to kiss her. She didn't have hair like Summer's, but that didn't mean the man wasn't wishing he could bury his hands in it.

Maybe it all was a line. Maybe she really was too gullible. And she couldn't confirm that his wife had cheated because he had said that he didn't tell anyone else. Maybe that was all a line too, and she couldn't even know that it was because there was no way to confirm or deny it, since he already admitted that no one else would know what she was talking about if she tried to talk to them about it.

"Thanks for your help. I understand if you need to go and want to run over and wrap your hands around someone's throat."

"His or hers?" Summer said with a laugh.

"Either? Both?" Sunny said, laughing along with her.

"It was my pleasure to help you. I appreciate having a place to come to when I needed it. You gave me just enough time for God to work His way in my life. And whatever is going on over there, whether it's just Gilbert doing what Mrs. Tucker asked or something more, I know that the Lord has a plan, I just need to...accept it." It was hard, since she did want to go and demand that he tell her whether he was sincerely enjoying himself or just acting like it. Couldn't he act like he was suffering?

She almost rolled her eyes at herself. If she were being forced to lead someone around town, introduce them to all the sights, and help them fall in love with the town so they bought a house nearby and spent their money in Mistletoe Meadows, to help all of her neighbors continue to make a living, she certainly would put her best effort into it and do everything she could to hide the fact that she hated what she was doing.

So, she could hardly blame him for appearing, for all intents and purposes, like he was enjoying himself.

The bell jingled, but she didn't turn around, throwing her apron in the basket and rearranging a few containers that had been knocked off the pile.

"Hello, Gilbert. Looks like you have a friend with you today."

"Hi, Sunny. This is Darla Zoubak. She's from DC and is looking to buy a weekend place here. I told her she could find the best muffins in town right here."

Summer continued to face the shelf, also realizing that the entire stack of containers was completely crooked and needed to be entirely restacked. She didn't want to turn around and face Gilbert. Even though he was right there. It was one thing to know in her head that he was doing exactly what he was supposed to be doing, it was another thing to be able to smile and pretend to be okay with it. She wasn't a very good actress.

"Well, thank you very much. Would you like to purchase a muffin so you can see that for yourself?" Sunny asked, and Summer could only imagine that Sunny was looking directly at Darla.

"Oh," Darla said, sounding flirtatious, "I think Gilbert was going to buy me one. He's been so charming and so knowledgeable about this sweet little town. He's just got my heart all aflutter with all of the amazing things that go on here."

Summer rolled her eyes as she stacked one more box on top of the other. Darla sounded like a simpleton. Maybe she was sounding that way on purpose, or maybe that was the way she talked when she was in a small town, condescending to the intelligence level she assigned to people who lived here.

That was not nice. She needed to be kind. God wanted her to be kind to everyone and not have these nasty thoughts in her head.

She took a breath and put another box up, stacking it as evenly and carefully as she could as Gilbert placed an order for two muffins.

Sunny moved along behind the counter, fulfilling their order, getting the coffees that he had requested as well, and she felt more than saw Gilbert shift.

"Summer?" he asked, and his voice sounded much closer. It seemed like he had moved down the counter and was leaning over directly behind where she knelt, putting the boxes away.

Now what was she going to do? She wasn't expecting him to call her out. She could hardly act like she didn't know he was there, but obviously she was being rude by ignoring him.

She turned but didn't straighten, looking up at him.

"Hey," she said.

"Hey. I just wanted to say hi. I...miss you."

"Gilbert, is this the girl you were talking about?" Darla came over and latched her arm around Gilbert's.

Summer's eyes dropped to her hand on his arm before she looked back up into Gilbert's face, which seemed to be pinched.

"The one who gave your children horseback riding lessons and worked in the bakery or something?"

So was he calling them lessons rather than therapy? Playing down the fact that she did have a degree, even though it might not be as spectacular as whatever Darla had. And she had just gone to a state school, nothing Ivy League or prestigious. Was Gilbert ashamed of her?

"Yes. She's the one that did the therapy with my children when my wife died. I credit her for their ability to bounce back so quickly and process everything in a healthy way."

"Oh, children are so resilient," Darla said, waving her hand.

"Sometimes they can be," Gilbert said, looking at Summer with his eyes narrowed as though he knew that there was obviously something wrong and was trying to figure out what it was.

Was he really that clueless?

She didn't think he probably was, but it didn't matter. Anyone who had a brain could figure out what her problem was and why, but anyone who called themselves a Christian should also not be acting the way she was.

"Darla, it's so nice to meet you," she said, rising and holding out her hand so she could shake Darla's.

Darla looked at it almost the way someone might look at a rat that all of a sudden appeared on the counter. But then, she slipped her long white fingers into Summer's work-roughened hand and shook it gingerly.

"It's nice to meet you," Darla said. "Gilbert didn't tell me that you were so short."

Summer thought about the four-inch heels that Darla wore. Probably the only set of four-inch heels in town, but Summer didn't say anything. Heels did not necessarily make a person bad. It was the attitude and the condescending manner that ruffled her feathers.

"I guess there's less of me to sit on the horse. I believe it's universal that horses typically like a light rider."

That wasn't the best comeback she'd ever had, but at least she was being kind.

Darla's laugh rang out. Although Summer didn't think that she had said anything funny.

"So I think Darla's going to get a muffin, and then my mother volunteered to show her anything else in town that she wanted to see. I was hoping that you'd be free to grab a Christmas tree. It'll be nice to be able to have it up so we can decorate it the day after Thanksgiving."

"Sure," she said before she could think about it and decline. She appreciated the fact that he must have called his mom to rescue him, and maybe she couldn't make it until just now, or maybe he felt like he needed to do a little bit of his duty before he had his mom take over. Still, whatever it was, it was obvious he was trying, and despite the little pain in her heart, she needed to meet him halfway.

Or maybe more. It felt like more, but regardless, she wasn't going to be unkind just because she hurt.

"You're going to decorate a tree together? Do you...live together?" Darla said. The question held surprise. Or maybe it was Darla's way of acting like she wasn't prying.

"I bought Summer's farm, and I asked Summer to move back in. She does her horse therapy business from the stables, and my children love her, and...so do I."

He had hesitated, but then he had admitted, in front of Darla, that he loved her. Maybe he just meant as a friend. It could definitely be construed that way, but at least he was defending her.

"Interesting. Well, small-town values are the same as values in DC." She lifted her shoulder, as though there was something wrong with them, and then walked back over to the cash register.

"Our muffins are ready." Her words were short and clipped where they weren't before.

"Sorry," she mouthed softly, knowing that Gilbert being nice to her had made Darla upset.

He shook his head. "You are the most important."

She gave a wan smile, because she appreciated the sentiment, and he had been kind to her, allowing Darla to be offended, but...it still hurt a little.

He walked away, and she turned back to the bunch of containers she was only half done stacking.

She acted like a junior high girl who didn't yet know how to get around in society. She wished she could go back and do it better.

I'm sorry, Lord. I flunked that test.

She felt like maybe God was not upset with her. That sometimes people just had to do things a couple of times before they got it right, and she could have done a lot worse.

Gilbert and Darla left the store, with Gilbert looking behind him once at her. She could see his reflection in the glass behind the counter that separated the counter area from the office.

She didn't turn around, but she liked the fact that he was looking anyway.

Not too long after that, his mom pulled up to the bench where they had sat back down, eating their muffins and drinking their coffee, and the three of them talked for a bit before Darla got in his mom's car and rode away.

By that time, Summer was finished stacking the containers, and she was just killing time until Darla left.

She needed to apologize to Gilbert.

Chapter Twenty-Three

*H*is mother couldn't drive away with Darla soon enough for him, Gilbert thought as her car slowly pulled out and he threw up a hand to wave before hurrying across the street.

He saw Summer standing in the doorway of Sunny's shop, and she didn't seem to be extremely angry, which made his heart slow down just a little bit. He had been afraid that she was furious with him, and he couldn't blame her. If he had looked out the window and seen some other man with his hand on her knee, he would have been hard-pressed not to go out and break the hand off.

"I'm sorry I wasn't very nice when you were in here just a few minutes ago," Summer said before he had even stopped in front of her.

"No. It's me. I'm sorry I continued to do what Mrs. Tucker asked me to do, even though I didn't want to. Then Darla was touching me, and I didn't know how to pick up her hand and throw it off me without being obvious about it. That's why I finally stood up and came over. I...had her sitting outside of the shop, just because I wanted to be close to you."

She closed her eyes for a moment and then smiled, shaking her head.

Finally she opened her eyes back up. "I wondered why you sat there. I wondered if you were just trying to rub it in that you are with someone else, and I knew that couldn't possibly be right, but it felt like that little bit."

"No way. Absolutely not. I... I showed her the town, as quickly as I could, but that kind of backfired on me, because then I didn't know what to do with her."

"Oh, that's terrible."

"I know. So that's how we ended up sitting there, and then finally I asked if she wanted a muffin, because that would get us standing up and get her fingers off me."

"All right, so beware if the man asks me if I want a muffin. He might possibly be wanting to get away from me."

"No. Not true." He reached a hand out like he was going to touch her cheek, and then it dropped, and he smiled a little guiltily. "I want to touch you, but we made those rules, and I kind of insisted on them."

"Yeah. I...thought about the rules and then thought about how unfair it was that Darla got to touch you and I wasn't allowed."

"Trust me. It wasn't because I wanted her to."

"Hey, you guys, why don't you take a muffin? Seems like you had a pretty big morning, and... Summer, what I said before? He's a good man," Sunny said, handing them both a blueberry muffin.

"Thank you," they said together as they each took a muffin out of her hands.

Gilbert waited until she left before he said, "What did she say earlier?"

"She was playing devil's advocate with me. Because I told her about you and me kissing and how we had decided to slow down and make sure that we were building a foundation that didn't necessarily include all the physical stuff right away."

"And how did she take that?"

"She warned me that you might be saying whatever you needed to in order to get what you wanted. And that I didn't know for sure that I could trust you, when I told her that I could."

She said it so simply, like she did just trust him without him needing to do anything to earn it.

"And then I sat down with Darla and her grippy hands, and made it look like your friend was right," he said as they opened their muffins and walked slowly along the street.

"Yeah. She did kind of hit me with that, but you came in, and I think when you talked to me in front of Darla, it convinced her that maybe I was right. Or she just thought about your reputation in town and realized that you didn't get that reputation by not being the kind of man you are."

"Well, whatever it was, I appreciate it." He nodded at his truck. "I really did want to take a ride with you. I figured if I'm driving and sitting on one side and you're over on the other side, it will be a little easier to just talk."

"I'm down for that. Although, I have horses that are supposed to be here this evening. I got that text just a little bit ago, but with all the other things... I was jealous. I'm sorry." She slowed down and then stopped, getting serious all of a sudden.

"I told you. I would have been jealous too. And probably a little violent. Unless I was able to get a hold of myself. I will work to try to make sure that never happens again."

"And I will work to make sure that I can be nice even when my heart hurts a little bit."

"I didn't mean to hurt you."

"I know. I know that. You know how you have head knowledge, but sometimes you just can't get your body's reactions to go along with what you know?"

"You have head knowledge that your feelings don't follow?" he said with a little smile.

"Yeah. Exactly." They both thought about the discussion that they'd had earlier about how they needed to acknowledge their feelings but not necessarily live by them.

He walked over to her side of the truck and opened the door.

He held out his hand so he could hold her muffin while she got in.

"Thank you."

"Sure," he said, having already finished his muffin. He'd lost his appetite a little bit while he was leading Darla around.

He walked around the front of the truck, after closing her door, and got in.

"That was about the worst morning I've had in a really long time," he said as he started his truck.

"It wasn't my favorite morning either, but I think we can put that behind us. I'm looking forward to the horses coming, and I know the kids are going to be excited about it."

"Can I thank you again for being so nice to my kids?" he asked as he looked in the rearview mirror. He turned his signal on and pulled out.

"Sure. Although, they're great kids. Of course I'm going to love them."

"Darla just acted like having kids was the worst thing. It reminded me that I needed to thank you for being kind about it. She...just went on about how kids were such a drag and how she was never going to have any, and she asked about their mother and whether we shared custody and all that."

"What'd you say to that?" Summer said with a laugh.

"I changed the subject. I didn't want to go into all that, because it's kinda complicated. Yes, she died. Then everybody gives me pity, then I feel guilty because I don't feel bad about it necessarily other than that my children lost their mom, which is hard to explain and I didn't want to talk about my personal life with Darla."

"Well, that makes me kind of happy. That you don't seem to have a problem talking about that with me."

"I told you. I feel comfortable with you, in a way that I don't feel with anyone else."

They started out along the street, then he pulled out onto the highway, intending to take her to the waterfall outside of town. It was a pretty place that he didn't visit nearly enough, and for some reason, he wanted to share it with Summer.

He had thought about it when he was taking Darla around, but for some reason, he didn't want to be there with her. Maybe because he had never been there with Summer. Whatever it was, he had just had such an urge to go with Summer that he could hardly wait to get her there.

"Where are we going anyway?" Summer asked, looking around as they drove outside of town in the opposite direction of the farm. She probably was confused.

"I was showing Darla around town, and I thought of the falls. I didn't want to take her there, and somehow all I could think about was getting you there with me."

"Really?" she asked, looking a little charmed, when he really hadn't meant to be charming. He just was being honest.

"Really." He didn't have any of the words. But he didn't seem to need them. She seemed happy, and her eyes glowed as she glanced at him, and then the falls came into view.

There was a short walk to get to the larger falls off the road, and he parked the truck in the designated area.

"Can we hold hands?" he asked as he walked around the truck and opened her door.

"That doesn't count as touching, does it?" she said as she hopped out, and he shut the door.

"I don't think so," he said, holding his hand out and watching as she slipped her fingers into his.

It felt good and right, not like the way it had felt when Darla had put her hand on his knee. He wanted to pull Summer closer, though, and he figured that holding hands was probably not a good idea either. But he wanted to have that connection. After the unstable morning that they'd had, which had been all his fault.

He shouldn't have put himself in a position where Darla could reach over and touch him, and he shouldn't have been afraid to move away from her hand, which would have given her the message that he didn't want her touch.

It would have been the thoughtful thing to do for Summer, and she would have been justified in her argument with her friend. Instead, he sat there and allowed Darla to do what she wanted, because he hadn't wanted to offend her.

He wished he could go back and do it over again, but he could learn from that, and not allow that type of thing to happen ever again, whether Summer was there to see it or not.

The trail was not difficult, and they moseyed back away from the road, from the little falls, and headed to the larger falls. There was an area set up where they could stand close to the falls and feel the water come down.

There was also a swimming hole at the bottom, but it was a little chilly for that.

"This is beautiful any time of year," Summer said, talking a little louder to be heard over the roar of the water. It wasn't a powerful waterfall, like a river, but it was still loud enough that talking softly was impossible.

"I agree. I've always loved coming here, and I haven't done it nearly enough. I don't even know if I've brought my kids here in the last year." Actually, he figured it had been several years since the kids and he had visited this, and considering how much they enjoyed seeing the falls and swimming in the swimming hole at the bottom over the summer, he couldn't believe he hadn't done it, except... His life had been a little upside down.

"I think you can be excused from that," Summer said, almost as though she had read his mind.

"I'd like to make up for those things. But you can't ever get the time back, you know?"

"I know. I have a few things I'd love to be able to go back and redo, but I can't."

"Like what?" he asked, sitting down on the bench and keeping a hold of her hand as she sat down beside him, their clasped hands resting between them.

"Like today. I wish I could have looked at that and known immediately that it wasn't what it seemed. I wish I could have said that confidently to Sunny and just trusted in your integrity."

"You don't know me that well. It's perfectly okay for you to question what you see, when you have no idea the depths of my character."

"But other people know your character." She shook her head. "Anyway. I want to do better."

"If Desire had gotten mad at me, she'd have been mad at me for at least a week and wouldn't have talked to me for three or four days, just to punish me, until I came to her, begging for forgiveness and half of the time not even knowing what it was I had done wrong."

She lifted her shoulder, as though unimpressed. Like being better than Desire wasn't exactly her goal.

He supposed that Desire didn't set a high bar, and Summer cleared it easily.

Regardless, he felt like he and Summer were doing things right.

Chapter Twenty-Four

"And then I just put them in the crockpot and turn it on low, and sometimes if I think about it, I might shuffle them around so they don't get too brown on one side, but if not, they'll be fine by the time it's time to eat."

Amy spoke to Summer and saw her listening attentively. She smiled. It was obvious that Summer wanted to learn how to make the filling balls so that she could fit into the family. Amy wasn't completely oblivious to the shy smile that moved between Summer and her brother Gilbert.

"I really appreciate you coming. You and Jones didn't have to spend your first Thanksgiving together here at our place, but it's definitely nicer to see someone make them than to just be handed a recipe."

"It's my pleasure. We usually hang out at Mom's house before the meal, so it wouldn't surprise me at all if the entire family is here by ten o'clock. I hope you're ready," Amy said with a laugh.

"Gilbert told me not to get excited about it. He said the family was very low-key, and you definitely made me feel at home."

"I'm glad about that," Amy said. "And Gilbert's right. We've had people coming in and out of our house for years. Ever since I can remember. Mom never told anyone no, and we were as likely as not to have someone new sitting at our table for any holiday or Sunday meal. Even a regular evening meal after school, we might have people there."

"Your mom is quite a lady," Summer said as she wiped off the table and threw the empty bread bags away.

"She sure is. I know I went through the typical teenage stage where I wanted to do everything the opposite of what Mom did, but that was short-lived. Nowadays, my main goal in life is to be half as good as what she is."

"That's a pretty high goal," Summer said, and they laughed together.

Larissa, who had been listening to them, said, "Can I call Grandma and see when she's coming?"

"You sure can, honey," Summer said.

Larissa left the room with Summer's phone.

"It's almost like they're yours," Amy said thoughtfully after she watched Summer hand Larissa her phone, not even needing to say her password, which Larissa already knew.

"Well, don't forget I had therapy with them once a week for a while, then went down to twice a month, but I still saw them an awful lot."

"And you always spent more time with them than you needed to," Amy said. "I'm not forgetting that."

She had admired Summer back then when Summer had been working with Gilbert's children, but she hadn't really put the two of them together. However, seeing them together in the house before Gilbert and Jones had taken the boys on out to the barn really made her think that perhaps Gilbert had finally found someone who appreciated the man he was. Amy had never really thought that he and Desire were the best couple, although she certainly would never tell her brother that he couldn't marry someone that he claimed to love.

"Hey, girlfriend," Jones said, sticking his head in.

"Hey yourself, husband," Amy said, wiggling her brows at him.

A look passed between them that felt as old as time but also new and different from the friendly looks that had passed between them all their lives.

"Gilbert wants to know if Summer will go down and help the boys ride horses before dinner. I told him that I'd send her down and stick around here and keep you company, even though it's a hardship," Jones teased.

Amy stuck her tongue out at him and said in a loud voice to Summer, "That man is incorrigible."

"That woman is gorgeous," Jones said, coming in and wrapping his arms around her.

Summer left without Amy even noticing as she twisted in Jones's arms until she had her arms around him and lifted his face so he could kiss her.

"Now that's what I'm talking about," Jones said as he lifted his head.

Amy felt her cheeks get warm, and she didn't know why. It wasn't like they hadn't been married for almost a year. Plus, they'd been best friends forever before that.

"Kissing you will never get old," she said, snuggling deeper into his arms and enjoying a little bit of privacy. It wasn't like their whole house wasn't private, since they didn't have any children, and Amy was a little bit sad about that. She kind of thought that they would start having children right away. But the money that they were supposed to have inherited from his aunt after they got married had never materialized. It turned out there had been some embezzling going on, and all the money from his aunt's estate had been needed to pay the bills. There was still some litigation going on, but Amy didn't figure they would ever see the money.

"You look sad," Jones said, and Amy again was amazed at how tuned into her moods he was.

"I'm not," she said, putting a smile on her face.

"Is it the money?"

"No. We're doing fine." And that was true. They had to move his practice, since the place where he had had it when they got married had been sold, but it actually worked out well because they were able to move it into the building right beside Amy's house. Where she kept her animal sanctuary. They had had to invest a little bit of money into redoing the building to contain exam rooms and a waiting room, and an operating table in the back, but they had done most of the work themselves, and their practice was busier than ever. Jones had let all the office help go, and he and Amy did everything.

Apparently people thought it was quaint that a married couple ran the veterinary practice together, and business was booming.

"You know we wouldn't be doing so well if it weren't for you," Jones said.

"Because people know how ferociously I love animals because they see what a crazy animal sanctuary I have?"

"No, because they love seeing a husband-and-wife team working together. And because they see how much you love their animals."

"All right. So I was half right."

"I can't even give you that much? Or you taunt me and lord it over me."

"I'd never," she said, swatting his arm lightly.

"When you do that, you know I have to kiss you to calm you down."

"Is that what happens," she murmured as his lips lowered again.

They didn't talk for a while, but Jones finally lifted his head and looked around the kitchen.

"These are nice digs," he said, admiring the spacious area and the high-class cabinetry and counters.

"They are, but I guess I would rather be with you than in a high-class kitchen all the time." She wasn't really much of a cook anyway. She could do it, because her mother had insisted she learn, but she preferred working with animals, and Jones did too. Sometimes her meals were rather lean.

"Have you seen the way Gilbert looks at Summer?" Jones asked, lifting his brows after he rested his forehead on hers.

"I have. Interesting, isn't it?"

"They really seem good together, although Summer seems so young compared to him. But she is a baby, and he's this old man with practically grown children."

"It is kind of amazing how quickly his kids have grown, isn't it?" The thought made her a little sad. Time marched on, unceasing, relentless, sometimes it felt like. She just wanted to freeze it and enjoy being young, but someday she'd look like her mother, and Jones would look like an old man beside her, and they'd be grandparents. If they ever had any children.

"There's that look again," Jones said.

"I don't have sad thoughts," Amy said, trying to summon up a happy smile.

"But it's Thanksgiving. You're supposed to have thankful thoughts," he said.

"I'm thankful for you. Thankful for my family. I'm thankful for the blessings that God gives me every day, that half the time I don't appreciate, and I know I should, because I'm so blessed."

"And I'm thankful for you. And I can say the same thing. God has blessed me far more than I deserve, that's for sure."

Amy snuggled in Jones's arms, thankful that his aunt had died and left them money, even though they'd never gotten it. If she hadn't done that, she and Jones might never have considered getting married, and she wouldn't be as happy as what she was right now, pressed against him, knowing that whether they had children, whether they didn't, whether their veterinary practice was a success or whether it wasn't, whether they got the money eventually or whether they didn't, it didn't matter.

She was one of the blessed people who had found the real deal. A man of character and convictions who would love her until he died.

Chapter Twenty-Five

Marjorie looked around the table, her heart overflowing with gratefulness.

"Let's pray," Gilbert said, and they all bowed their heads. She listened to her son's voice rumble a short but heartfelt prayer to the Lord. And her whole soul echoed her gratefulness. She never dreamed when she got married that it would end up like this, with her husband passing away so early and her ending up raising her children alone. She worried every day whether she would be able to raise them to love and serve the Lord. That had been her whole effort and desire. Sure, she wanted them to be able to work and to make a living, but even that was secondary to knowing the Lord and loving Him. There wasn't anything that was more important.

"Amen," Gilbert said, and the whole table echoed, "Amen."

They started passing dishes, and Marjorie watched as her children helped their children with some of the dishes. Isadora, down on the end, had a child in the high chair beside her, another one on the other side in a booster seat, and her oldest, all of four years old, sitting at the table directly beside that child.

Isadora had had a fairly difficult year, but she had confided to

Marjorie recently that she was almost glad that God allowed it to happen. She had grown closer to the Lord and learned to depend on Him in ways that she never would have if her husband hadn't cheated and left her for someone else.

Of course, not long ago, he'd come back, asking her to take him back, and she had considered it for a while, because she wanted her children to know their father, but in the end, she said no. He left, and she wasn't going to take that chance again.

Marjorie was secretly very pleased, mostly because her ex had not come to the Lord, he just wanted Isadora back because she had been an excellent wife and had put up with almost everything he dished out. He hadn't found a woman who was as godly and forgiving as Isadora, and basically he just wanted someone who was going to stroke his ego.

It was true that Isadora had been an excellent wife, even though at times Isadora felt like she was a failure. But Marjorie was almost certain that there was another man out there somewhere who God had for her daughter. Someone who would appreciate her for what she was and who she was.

Her ex had no intention of staying true, and Marjorie could see that from a mile away. Thankfully, Isadora had either figured that out, or God had protected her. One of the two.

Regardless, Marjorie hoped that the coming year would see Isadora making even more strides toward becoming the woman that God wanted her to be.

"Look at these beets, Mom. Looks like Summer might be giving you a run for your money," Roland said as he handed the Harvard beets around to her.

"I don't care who makes them. This is my favorite vegetable ever," she said as she gave herself a generous portion. Beets were good for a person, although there was a good bit of sugar in Harvard beets, and she supposed that that negated most of the healthy benefits. Although, they would probably be better for her than the stuffing balls which she also loved.

She made sure to take some of them as they went around, because Amy had told her that Summer had helped to make them, and Marjorie didn't want to hurt Summer's feelings.

She looked at Summer, who was saying something low to Gilbert who sat beside her.

Larissa sat on one side of Summer, and Robert sat on the other side of Gilbert, but there was no child between them.

Marjorie wondered if there might be something going on there.

She looked across the table at Lucas who was stuck like glue to Judd's side. Judd had married her oldest daughter, Terry, and Marjorie felt like that was a match made in heaven.

Although Terry had confided to Marjorie that they wanted to have children and hadn't been able to.

Marjorie had patted her arm and told her not to worry about it. It had been less than a year, and sometimes people waited far longer than that to get pregnant, but internally she worried. Terry was older, and maybe they wouldn't ever be able to have children, which was a shame. All the people who had kids and didn't care about them, and there was Terry and Judd who would make excellent parents.

Not to mention, her heart bled at Terry's sorrow over the fact that getting pregnant had not been easy.

Still, lots of people went through harder things, and in every other way, Terry and Judd were doing fantastic. They were so obviously in love, and they cared for each other so well. They also spent a lot of time with her nieces and nephews, which was one of the main reasons why Terry had moved back.

Her eyes went again to Summer and Gilbert. Maybe there would be another wedding in their future.

"Mom, are you gonna pass the beets or not?" Roland said from beside her. Roland, her youngest, wasn't quite ready to get married yet. Although, she suspected that he was more mature than he let on. The youngest sometimes had trouble growing up, since they were so used to everyone treating them like a baby.

Conversation flowed easily around the table, the food was delicious, and it was one of the best Thanksgivings that Marjorie could remember. Of course, she thought that every year. Because her heart always overflowed with gratitude. The good was always better than the bad. Even the lean years, where she wasn't sure where the money for Christmas was going to come from, or whether she was going to be able to continue to pay the mortgage or not. God had always been good, and He provided so abundantly that if she thought about it too much she'd tear up and embarrass everyone at the table.

"All right, guys, we have some really good desserts, including pumpkin pie, pumpkin roll, and chocolate cake." Gilbert paused while there were cheers from the kids. Probably over the chocolate cake, and Marjorie hid a smile. She had decided that she'd be a little different and make a more traditional dessert for their Thanksgiving meal, to go along with everything pumpkin. It appeared that it was a pretty good idea.

"But before that, I have a bit of an announcement to make." Gilbert looked down at Summer, and Marjorie held her breath. These things could go either way. He might be going to announce that they were expecting a baby, and while she would be happy for them, it wasn't her ideal.

Immediately she shook the thought aside. She needed to have faith in her children and faith that God had filled in the gaps if she hadn't raised them right. Surely they would want to please Him, and that would be their main concern.

She hoped so.

"Summer and I are...courting, I guess. We're not dating, and we're looking to get married before Christmas."

Marjorie's eyes went to the children sitting on either side of them, and their eyes shone. It seemed like they might have already talked to the kids about it, so there weren't any surprises at the table. Marjorie was impressed that the kids could keep that kind of a secret.

"We know that's kind of fast, and we know the town's going to be talking. Especially because Summer is living here. So, we kind of were keeping it under wraps for a bit. I wanted to give her time to get to know me so that she can decide whether she can put up with me or not."

"You know it's the other way around," Summer said, poking him in his side.

He caught her hand and threaded his fingers through hers.

Marjorie smiled at the sweet gesture.

"It's so that she can make sure that she wants to put up with me. You guys all know that," Gilbert said, earning a chorus of, "yeah, we know," around the table.

"Thanks, guys," Gilbert said, rolling his eyes.

He waited for everything to die back down before he said, "I just wanted you guys to know, and then I also wanted to ask if you guys could just kinda keep it on the down-low until you hear that she and I have announced it. Which...it won't be too long. Unless she kicks me to the curb."

"Get away while you still can, girl," Roland called.

If Marjorie were his sister, she would have poked him in the side, but instead, she just shook her head. She had to say something in defense of her son.

"You're getting a good man, Summer. Gilbert is a wise choice."

Summer smiled at her and nodded, and Marjorie had the feeling that Summer didn't need her to tell her what a good man Gilbert was. It looked like she already knew.

"That was a nice defense, Mom," Gilbert said to her, smiling.

"Dad is the best," Larissa said, looking up with admiration in her eyes at her father.

Marjorie smiled too. Larissa was still at the age where she idolized her dad. She hoped she would never grow out of it, although the polish always became tarnished a little as a person grew older, and a child became a teenager and then a young adult. They realized their parents weren't perfect and did indeed have faults. But hopefully, they came back around and realized that everyone had faults, and that their parents had done the best they could.

Her kids had all gone through that to some extent, and she thought that all of them had come back around and didn't demonize her, but realized that she'd done the very best she could.

She looked forward to the happy Christmas season ahead, even though she knew that every year nothing ever went as planned.

There would be squabbles and heartbreak, problems and issues, but the good would always outweigh the bad, because God would see to it.

She thought about the doctor's report that she had just gotten back and wondered how that would play into things in the coming year. She had determined in her heart that she wasn't going to think about it over the holiday nor allow it to ruin anyone's celebration, so she quickly pushed it aside.

Life was good.

Chapter Twenty-Six

"Wow. What a day," Summer said, practically falling down onto the swing from sheer exhaustion.

"I know my family can be a little much," Gilbert said as he sat down beside her, a good six inches or so away.

She appreciated him putting down some guidelines and following them, but right now was one of those times where she would like to just crawl into his side and cuddle there.

She was so tired her bones ached, but after they put the kids to bed, he had suggested that they come down and sit on the swing for a bit, and she had consented immediately. Anything to be able to spend some time with him. They hadn't been alone together all day.

"Do you think you're going to be able to handle that?" he asked easily.

He didn't tell her, but she saw it as an opening to conversation.

"I know I am. You're well-liked among your siblings."

"And I like them. And they loved you."

"They just like teasing you about me putting up with you. That seemed to be the favorite subject of the day."

"Maybe you should take it a little more seriously than what you are. I might be harder to get along with than what you think."

"I'll take my chances. I appreciate your character and your integrity. If you're a little bit stubborn or grumpy, I'll handle that and take that over a cheater any day."

"You will never have cause to call me a cheater," Gilbert said with certainty.

She knew that was true. Everyone had their faults, but that was not one of his, and it wasn't one of hers either.

"Do you think you're going to have enough energy to put the tree up tomorrow?" he asked.

"I think after I have a good night's sleep, I'll be able to be more enthusiastic about my yes."

He laughed. "I can do it, or we can wait. I don't want to force you into something you don't want."

"Oh, I definitely want it. This is a fun time of year, and I know the kids are going to enjoy it."

"I've been meaning to ask you if you left decorations up in the attic. I had seen there was a whole pile of stuff up there but didn't go through any of it. And I know this is terrible, but I left all the decorations I had with Desire in the house when I sold it. I just didn't have the gumption to go through all that stuff, not to mention I didn't have anywhere to keep it."

"Well, that's a good thing, because I did the same thing when I sold the house. I left all the Christmas decorations right where they are. Up in the attic, packed away."

"Perfect. I think you and I are more alike than what we think."

"Maybe, maybe not," she said, her eyes twinkling at him. He seemed to see that in the dark, and he laughed. She was thinking about the fact that they weren't the slightest bit alike, since he was a man and she was a woman, and maybe he didn't get that, but he got the gist of it.

"Daddy?" a voice said, and Summer squinted through the darkness to the door as a white figure came out.

Larissa in her nightgown.

"Can I sit with you guys for a little bit?"

"You sure can," he said, and Summer slid over so that Larissa could climb up between them.

"Daddy?"

"Yes, sweetie?"

"Is it bad that I was happier today, with the horse rides and with helping Summer cook, than I was the last time we had Thanksgiving with Mommy?"

Gilbert was quiet for a moment, and Summer waited to see what he would say. Sure, she had some counseling training, but at times like this, there might not be any right answer, or there might be several. But the idea was to let her feel what she needed to feel while knowing how to act correctly.

"I think that's just fine," Gilbert said. "I don't want you to take this wrong, but I like today better too. Although, maybe it's something that happens as you get older, but every year, I think on Thanksgiving that it's my favorite Thanksgiving ever. Does that make sense?"

"Not really," Larissa said, scrunching up her nose and wiggling deeper between them.

Summer reached over and took a hold of her hand, and Larissa grabbed it back, threading their fingers together and holding tight.

"Summer is nice to snuggle with."

"I agree with that," Gilbert said, sounding cautious.

"But I still miss Mommy," Larissa said.

"I think that's normal," Gilbert said.

Summer noticed that he didn't say that he missed her too. He'd already told her more than once that he really didn't, although he wasn't glad she had died. Of course not. And he felt guilty because at times he thought that that would have been a good solution. But he didn't mean to make it so.

She knew that the guilt would probably be with him forever. After all, when a person wished something horrible, and then that horrible thing came to pass, the person couldn't help but feel guilty and somehow responsible. It was human nature.

That's why Summer would always caution people to be very careful about what they wish for, because a person never knew when it might actually happen.

They sat on the swing, pushing back and forth, and finally Larissa said, sounding a little bit more sleepy, "I want to keep taking therapy from Summer. Even though she lives with us. I liked it when she let us work with horses."

"I'm sorry. That's my fault. The horses came back this week, and I was busy with other things. But I'll make sure that we have therapy at least once a week, because I think the horses missed you guys too. Especially Cricket." Summer spoke softly, knowing what she said was true. Cricket did really seem to be happy to see Larissa when she got off the trailer.

"If I save up my money, can I buy Cricket?"

"Yes," Summer said before Gilbert could say anything.

"We'll have to be careful. Summer might not be able to sell her therapy horses. She might need them to give other little girls therapy."

"I have other horses, and maybe it's about time that I buy another one and work on training it to be good with little girls. I think Cricket has almost earned her retirement from therapy, and she would like to be your horse forever."

"How long do horses live?" Larissa asked, her voice slurring a bit.

"They can live to be in their twenties. Some horses even live to be thirty."

"How old is Cricket?"

"The vet said she's about 18 or so. It's hard to tell for sure, and I didn't have her when she was born, so I don't know. Just like you can't know how old I am by looking at me. You can make a guess, but unless you know my birthday, you don't know for sure."

Larissa's deep breathing showed that she had fallen asleep while Summer was talking.

Summer met Gilbert's eyes over the head of their little girl. They smiled at each other, and they sat on the swing for another few minutes until they were sure that she was asleep.

"I'll be right back," Gilbert said, picking her up and having Larissa stir a little before she snuggled into his arms, and he carried her into the house.

Summer had gotten up to hold the screen door so that it didn't slam shut behind him.

The warm weather had held, and it was a beautiful night to be outside. A beautiful night to be with people she loved, a beautiful night to be alive. She wasn't sure if she'd ever been happier in her life before.

It seemed like no time at all that Gilbert came back down, but instead of settling himself back on the swing, he knelt on one knee in front of her, holding a little box.

"I know I said I was going to wait, but I saw this in the window of the jewelry store when I was with Darla, and I sent her in for ice cream while I picked it out and paid for it. I...was still going to wait, but today was a perfect day for me. I couldn't have said it better than Larissa. Being with you is so much better than being with Desire. I... don't want to talk badly about her, and you know that, but I know that I'm older, and wiser, and I love you, and I'm messing this up terribly, but would you marry me?"

He was quiet after that, and Summer wanted to laugh and cry at the same time. He was so sweet, so perfect. Sure, he didn't exactly have a great speech planned, and maybe he was doing this spur of the moment, but there was nothing she would rather have than a starry night, the warm satisfaction of spending time with family, eating good food, having good fellowship, and knowing that the man she loved loved her and wanted to marry her.

"Yes," she said.

"Thank you. You're giving me a heart attack there. I thought you were trying to figure out a nice way of letting me down."

"Never. I was just thinking about how perfect this is."

"That was the worst marriage proposal ever. I just...didn't want to wait. I want to get married as soon as you are willing."

"I think it would be sweet to have a small wedding, because I think Larissa would love being a bridesmaid, and I would love having her."

"And how long do you think it's going to take to put something like that together?" he asked, pulling the ring out of the box and sliding it onto her finger.

She admired it in the moonlight and shook her head. "No time at all. We don't have to have anything fancy for it. Just...some flowers, I guess."

"If you want a bigger wedding, we can do it. I know it's my second wedding, but you only get one first wedding, and I want it to be everything you want."

"I have dreams about Christmas. Dreams about having a big family together and enjoying all the hubbub and craziness that big families have on Christmas. But those are the only dreams I have. Christmas dreams. Not wedding dreams."

"All right then. You name the day, and I'll be there."

"Two weeks?"

"That sounds good to me."

She figured out what day that would be and what the date would be. A Thursday evening seemed perfect. "All right then. I'll get everything together, and you just need to show up."

"May I kiss you, to celebrate our engagement?"

"You can kiss me anytime," she said, the warmth and love that she felt practically bursting from her.

"Well, I think it might be a good idea to be careful, but I think a small kiss to celebrate our engagement might be in line."

"I think I can be ready to be married next week this time," she said, after he had kissed her for what felt like forever but not nearly long enough.

"Hmm. Maybe a second kiss will convince her that tomorrow is better."

"How about you kiss me and see if that works?" she said with a smile as his lips descended on hers once more.

Chapter Twenty-Seven

"You look pretty," Larissa said as she stood beside Summer, near the falls outside of town.

"Thank you. You're very beautiful," Summer said, looking with pride at the little girl who looked up at her, her hands in Summer's, and their dresses, while not the same color or style, were similar colors. Dark blue with orange tones.

It seemed to fit the fall theme.

"I hear the music," Summer said.

Just as she said that, Terry hurried back toward them.

"You girls are beautiful," Terry said with a smile. Then she looked at Summer. "Gilbert's waiting. Jones is standing beside him and hoping that you'll hurry getting out there, because he's scared to death Gilbert's going to faint, and Jones is going to have to catch him so he doesn't fall in the water."

"Boy. That would make for a memorable wedding," Summer said, concerned.

"Don't worry. I told Gilbert to breathe, to take deep breaths, hold them, and blow them out. I think he'll be okay, it's just that I'm actually worried about Jones now."

Summer laughed.

"Are you ladies ready?" Amy said as she came up the path. They couldn't see the guests that were there, not that there were many. Just Gilbert's family and a few people from church.

Everyone was invited to the reception afterward, at the farm. They had picnic tables set up, and Marjorie, bless her heart, had big tubs of food ready to feed an army.

For her sake, Summer hoped people showed up. Cricket and Bunny would be hitched to the wagon, and they would be giving rides. She thought it would probably feel more like a carnival than a wedding reception, but she was okay with that. She wanted people to be celebrating. This was a happy day for her.

"I think we are, aren't we?" Summer looked down at Larissa, who nodded her head.

Lucas and Robert were standing beside their dad, Judd, and Jones.

Sunny and her string trio were providing the music, and it sounded like the song that they were supposed to walk out to.

"All right. Isadora is waiting to take pictures, because no one takes pictures like she does," Amy said as she and Terry hurried back.

"Looks like it's just you and me, kiddo," Summer said, looking down at Larissa.

"Does this mean that you're going to be my mom?" Larissa asked, and Summer wondered if she'd been waiting to ask that question until things died down. It seemed like it had been nonstop activity since Thanksgiving. But they'd gotten their tree up, it had been beautiful, and it was possible that she and Gilbert had kissed beside it. Although, they really had tried to be circumspect. After all, both of them wanted to honor the Lord, and with the wedding so close, it was easier to wait.

"If you want me to be." Summer took a breath, her heart swelling. She loved this little girl so much, but she didn't want her to forget her real mom. Even though her mom had cheated on her dad and maybe wasn't the upright character that her daughter had in her mind, she was still her mother, and she deserved love and respect.

"I love Mommy, but...she's not here anymore. And I really want you to be my mom."

"All right. How about we can both be your mom? You have your mommy that you had up until you were nine, and then you have me, and I'll be your mom for the rest of your life."

"Are you going to die too?" Larissa asked, and while Summer didn't want to make everyone wait on her, and she didn't want the musicians to have to play their piece twice, she felt like it was more important to spend time alleviating Larissa's fears.

"Everyone dies. Everyone. You, me, everyone. But if we know Jesus, if we've accepted him as our Savior, then we'll spend eternity in heaven. Right now, your mommy is up in heaven waiting on you to get there. She's probably a little bit lonely without you, although I'm sure she wants you to live a good full life living for the Lord down here. I wish I could tell you that I'm not going to die anytime soon, but the reality is, only God knows. But if I do, you'll know for sure that I'll be standing right beside the gate, waiting for you to walk through. And if I'm allowed, I'm going to peek down and watch your life, and see you live for the Lord while I'm waiting for you. Okay?"

"I think so."

"And your mommy and I will be really good friends," Summer said.

"Do you like her?" Larissa asked.

"I never met her, but I know that when I do, I will love her, because we both love you."

Larissa smiled big, and her fears seemed to be gone.

Summer wasn't so naïve as to believe that they would never come back, but she did know that there were things that Larissa could know were true, and they would help her be able to grapple with the harder facts of life.

"Are you okay?" Summer asked, hearing the musicians start the song again. And seeing Amy leaning over, looking down the trail.

Summer waved, indicating that everything was okay, and then she looked down at Larissa.

"I'm fine. I'm happy."

"All right. If you're ready to walk down, it sounds like they're ready for you. You have the rings?"

Larissa reached in the little pouch that she had on her wrist. "I have both of them."

"Perfect. You go on, I'll be right behind you. Don't walk too fast. I don't want to trip. I'm not used to wearing heels."

They weren't huge heels. They were square and serviceable, because she would be walking in the woods. She wanted to wear something a little bit dressy. But not so fancy that she looked completely out of place. Still, the waterfall was the perfect backdrop, and she wanted to wear something that complemented it.

Of course, nothing was as important as the man who stood at the end of her walk, in front of the pastor, and right beside his sons. Who looked at her as she walked slowly around the bend. She moved toward his family and the man who loved her.

Leaves fell down around her as a gust of wind blew over, and she was thankful for the little jacket she wore with her dress, since there was a bit of a chill in the air.

Still, she couldn't ask for a better day for early December, although it didn't matter. She would have gotten married no matter what the weather and been thankful for it.

Gilbert couldn't seem to take his eyes off her, and he looked at her with such love and devotion that it was all she could do to walk sedately and not run to him and put her arms around him.

To think that would be hers for the rest of her life, to hug him whenever she wanted to, to touch him as much as she cared to, and to get to hear everything he had to say, and to tell him her every thought, if she chose to.

To give her life to him, to serve him, and to do her best to make his life easier and happier and brighter. While he did the same for her.

Yeah, it would have been extremely difficult for anyone to wipe the smile off her face.

Chapter Twenty-Eight

Roland McBride watched the horses as they went in front of him once more.

He was the only one of his family that hadn't gotten married, and while he didn't exactly feel left out, he did wonder if maybe there was something wrong with him.

"Hey, Roland," Judd said, sitting down beside him.

"Hey there, Judd," he said, respect in the line of his body as he shifted to make room for Judd. Terry, his oldest sister and the sibling that he most looked up to, had chosen a good man. Judd was quiet, but as they said, still waters ran deep, and there was a lot about Judd to learn about, and everything that he learned showed him what a great man he was.

Roland felt a little guilty that he had squandered so much of his life, when he saw how much Judd had done.

Of course, it was never too late to get started working for the Lord, and Roland had a few things in mind.

"You enjoying the wedding?"

"The food is good, so I'm happy."

"You're not gonna talk about how beautiful the bride is or how in love your brother looks?" Judd said, teasing a little.

"That's probably all true, but my stomach is happy, and so am I."

"Well, that's good, because I have a favor to ask of you."

"All right?"

"Don't you think you ought to hear it before you agree?"

"I was agreeing to hear it, not to do it," Roland said, knowing that Judd was just teasing him.

"So you probably heard about the Secret Saint, he goes around town doing good deeds."

"I have." He had no idea who it was, but he knew his family had benefited from it at times. Last year, when Desire had been in the hospital dying of cancer, no one had been thinking about gifts for Gilbert's children, but the Secret Saint had somehow managed to get gifts underneath the Christmas tree.

The Secret Saint had also helped Charity, his sister-in-law, with gifts for her children too, before his brother Wilson had married her.

Wilson and Charity were riding in the carriage now, together, with no children. Charity was expecting again, and Wilson rode with one hand behind her, one hand on her stomach, as though to protect her.

Roland shook his head at how silly love could make a man behave.

"I wanted to know if you were interested in helping the Secret Saint."

Roland blinked and looked at Judd. "You know who it is?"

Judd nodded. "You know it's a secret. So, you're going to have to agree to help before I can tell you who it is."

Roland looked down at his hands. He wanted to help, but... It seemed like a lot of work, and he didn't understand how the Secret Saint knew all the things he knew. Like who needed help, and what to do for them. Somehow he seemed to know when people were behind on their mortgage, or needed money for their light bill, or needed their oil tank filled, and all kinds of things like that. The

Secret Saint seemed to know things in town that no one else knew. It was pretty amazing how he moved in perfect time with everything, and then as Roland was thinking about it, he thought, what better person than a doctor to find out who needed things?

"Is my sister the Secret Saint?" he asked, referring to Judd's wife, Terry.

"Are you agreeing to help?" Judd asked evenly, not forgetting the words that he had said.

Roland thought about it. He had just been thinking that he wanted to do more for the Lord, and maybe this was God opening a door. Sometimes it seemed like God dragged His feet and tested his patience, taking His good old time in answering his prayers, but in this case, he barely thought it before opportunity materialized. Unless he was making a mountain out of a molehill.

"Yes. I agreed to help."

"All right, then. Here's what you need to know."

Join Jessie's list and be the first to know about new releases and sales on her books!

Read Holly Jolly Dreams, the next book in the Mistletoe Meadows series (Coming in Fall 2025!) following Roland McBride as he takes of the Secret Saint duties in Mistletoe Meadows. But when a competitor shows up in the form of Nelly Bushnell, his sworn enemy, the sparks that start flying might just be fireworks in disguise.

A Gift from Jessie

View this code through your smart phone camera to be taken to a page where you can download a FREE ebook when you sign up to get updates from Jessie Gussman! Find out why people say, "Jessie's is the only newsletter I open and read" and "You make my day brighter. Love, love, love reading your newsletters. I don't know where you find time to write books. You are so busy living life. A true blessing." and "I know from now on that I can't be drinking my morning coffee while reading your newsletter — I laughed so hard I sprayed it out all over the table!"

Claim your free book from Jessie!

Escape to more faith-filled romance series by Jessie Gussman!

The Complete Sweet Water, North Dakota Reading Order:

Series One: Sweet Water Ranch Western Cowboy Romance (11 book series)

Series Two: Coming Home to North Dakota (12 book series)

Series Three: Flyboys of Sweet Briar Ranch in North Dakota (13 book series)

Series Four: Sweet View Ranch Western Cowboy Romance (10 book series)

Spinoffs and More! Additional Series You'll Love:

Jessie's First Series: Sweet Haven Farm (4 book series)

Small-Town Romance: The Baxter Boys (5 book series)

Bad-Boy Sweet Romance: Richmond Rebels Sweet Romance (3 book series)

Sweet Water Spinoff: Cowboy Crossing (9 book series)

Small Town Romantic Comedy: Good Grief, Idaho (5 book series)

True Stories from Jessie's Farm: Stories from Jessie Gussman's Newsletter (3 book series)

Reader-Favorite! Sweet Beach Romance: Blueberry Beach (8 book series)

Blueberry Beach Spinoff: Strawberry Sands (10 book series)

From Strawberry Sands to: Raspberry Ridge (12 book series)

Swoonfully Jolly Holiday Stories:

Holiday Romance: Cowboy Mountain Christmas (6 book series)

Cowboy Mountain Christmas Spinoff: A Heartland Cowboy Christmas (9 book series)

New and Much Loved: Mistletoe Meadows (4 books and counting!)

Laughing Through the Snow: Christmas Tree, PA Sweet Romcoms (6 short reads)